AMERICAN PIE

AMERICAN PIE

Michael Baughman

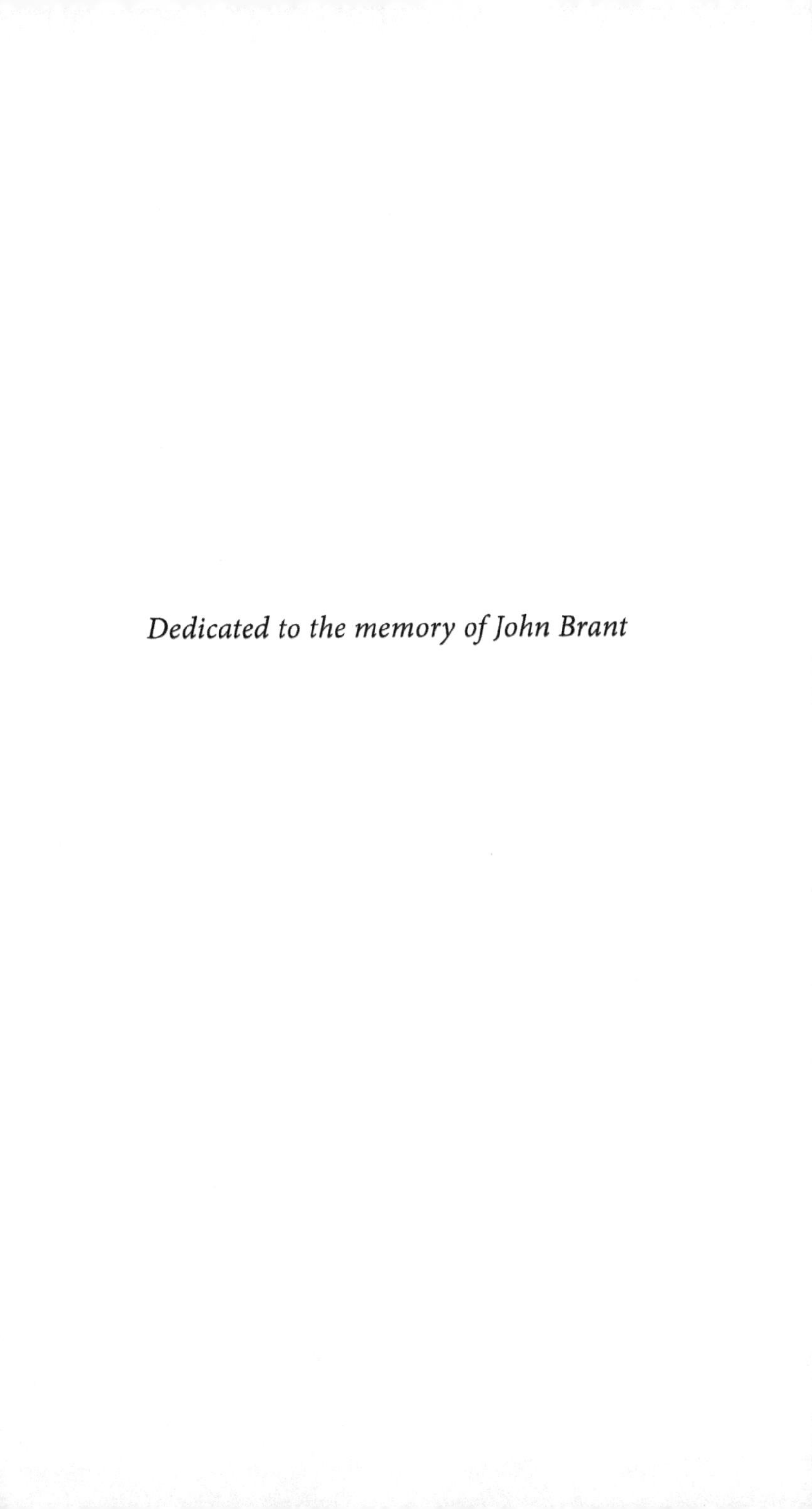

Dedicated to the memory of John Brant

Collective fear stimulates herd instinct, and tends to produce ferocity toward those not regarded as members of the herd.

—Bertrand Russell

Note

I've been writing for a long time – short stories, essays, articles, books – and through the years have worked with editors all the way from New York City to Honolulu. Often they've improved my work, sometimes not. Every editor and agent who read the American Pie manuscript urged me to make revisions relevant to characterization and dialogue they believed would offend specific groups of people. Even if that's true, in point of fact there have always been and always will be people everywhere who deserve to be offended. That's why I'm publishing what could be my last book independently.

CONTENTS

PART ONE

White Lightning 1

＊·＊

PART TWO

The Clever Raccoon 105

PART ONE
WHITE LIGHTNING

Otro

Wild country was indelibly written in Otro's blood. After seeing enough of the world he settled in a remote portion of the Pacific Northwest, where he earned a sufficient living by guiding hunters and anglers. Most of his clients were purportedly successful men, many of whom displayed a need to periodically escape their wearisome lives.

Every October Otro took a client named Norman Angell to an isolated high-elevation trout stream. Angell was a middle-aged and highly placed advertising executive employed by a company that manufactured sex toys and had begun preparations to market high-tech sex dolls. On the third night of their first outing together Otro and Angell faced one another across a campfire, and, as usual, Angell was drunk. "Do you understand how big business works?" he asked Otro. "Advertising's the driving force. Always has been. Always will be too. Well maybe I'm vain, but I'm damn successful. I shit you not, I earn a hell of a lot of money. Yeah, a *shit*load of money! But I *hate* my work. De*spise* it. Why? 'Cause I believe in love. I really do! Okay, I admit it, I'm old-fashioned. A romantic. A puritan maybe even. Way behind the times. I admit it. But I want a wife. Children to love. But none of the women I meet at church and get to know and actually like, the kind I want for a wife, they never want to *see* me again, not after they find out what I do for a living. I know I'm not very good-looking. Kind of fat too I guess. People I know joke about it. My friends do. Are they really friends? Tell me the truth. Am I fat?"

"No," Otro lied.

"I'll tell you how I'll become a bigger so-called success than I already am. I hate the idea but the goddamn gospel truth is that high-tech sex dolls are the future. You wait, you'll see for yourself. Before too many more years go by we'll be right where I predict. We're already promoting the idea, the possibility. Laying out our plans. Someday before too long, sooner or later, sooner maybe, I hope, a customer'll be able to order up a doll exactly like he or she wants it. Every physiological detail, from hair to breasts – for the female bot that would be - to genitals to toenails. The important point, the critical point, hell, it's obvious, or should be. Sexbots not only won't age, they'll never ever argue or complain about anything or never get jealous or irritable. Never talk until they're spoken to, thanks to AI that is. You know what AI is? Artificial Intelligence? It's been around since the damn 1950s. It's going wild now. Anyway, when sex dolls do talk they'll always say something pleasant, friendly, sexy when the time's right. So why should anybody put up with a pain in the ass human husband or wife? Kids is the only reason, right? Okay, adopt! Somebody'll be making adoptable kids somewhere! Anyway, goddamn it, I *hate* what I do, what I'm doing, and I goddamn hate myself for doing it! And I want a wife! And my own damn kids!"

Angell's corporation granted him two month-long vacations per year. For his winter month he camped with a cousin on a South Pacific island. He spent most of his fall month camping with Otro. Out in the wild, the two of them lived on freshly killed and gathered food: grouse, mountain quail, occasional rattlesnakes, edible plants and berries. Sitting at their campfire after dinner every night, Angell wore a cowboy hat and drank his straight rye whiskey from an antique tin cup. During their second year together he began admitting to Otro that his angling journeys were "attempts to cleanse his rotted out soul." He said it nearly every night, sometimes weeping as he spoke.

On one of their expeditions, when the two of them were less than halfway from the trailhead to what Otro called Bereavement Creek, a powerful wind and rain storm forced them to shelter themselves overnight in a cave. There were Indian bowls and pestles in the cave, and, in lantern light, Otro dug a few inches into the packed earthen floor with his hunting knife and un-covered obsidian fragments along with a few arrow and spear points. The artifacts brought a smile to his face. He handled them for a while before dropping them into one of the stone bowls.

"Hey, okay if I take one of those arrowheads for a souvenir?" Angell asked.

"No, don't," Otro answered.

"Are you some kind of Indian? Is that where your name comes from? I mean, you only use that one name, right?"

Because Angell seemed even drunker than usual, Otro was sure he'd forget whatever he heard, so told him more than he usually revealed about himself. "Years ago I decided to name myself," he said. "Otro – meaning Other in Spanish - was the word I chose from among the languages I know."

"How the hell'd you learn languages? How many do you know?"

"Only five."

Angell shrugged his shoulders without making an answer, a bewildered look on his pale, pudgy face.

The storm had passed by morning, but because of Angell's cruel hangover they got off to a late start. Two mornings later, high in rugged country, they reached the creek. Otro organized their camp on a nearly level space in a grove of stunted lodgepole pines on the flank of an extinct volcano.

They were lucky with the weather. For two weeks, day and night, they had calm winds under an overcast sky. With Otro's patient help, day after day, using arti-ficial flies tied on barbless hooks, Angell hooked and landed rainbow trout, and he exalted in it. All the fish were released unharmed until the final day, when Otro killed and gutted three hook-jawed males. He packed them in a portable cooler back to the trailhead, where his old Ford Bronco was parked beside Angell's Mercedes sedan.

Angell thanked Otro with tears in his eyes. "You're a weird man," he said. "Weird, but good. You look pretty tough too. Damn tough I guess. I guarantee I'll never give you any grief. Well then! Thanks for the damn fish! See you next year!"

>-<

Late that night, driving toward home, a sudden gust of howling wind drove a powerful surge of rain into Otro's windshield. He had no choice but to stop alongside the road and wait it out.

All night long the Bronco shuddered in wind gusts and the volume of hammering rain never let up. Lying on his side on the back seat, Otro slept until morning. In a recurring dream he saw the Oglala Lakota Sioux warrior Crazy Horse at Little Big Horn. Crazy Horse had his father's name and his mother's name was Rattle Blanket Woman. At Little Big Horn there were thick clouds of brown dust and white smoke from gunfire and rifle reports and pounding hoofs and screams. He saw George Armstrong Custer sprawled out flat on his back, scalped and dead, his seeping blood turning the powdery brown dust black.

In his dream Otro knew that throughout his life Crazy Horse cared little for tribal customs and traditions. Whenever possible, he preferred to hunt and wander the prairies alone. When he wanted or needed to be with people he rarely looked them in the eye and seldom spoke. He dressed simply and wore a single feather into battle, and never allowed himself to be photographed. Among his people he was known and loved for helping the poor, the sick, and the helpless.

In 1877, at age thirty-four, Crazy Horse was arrested by soldiers and taken to Fort Robinson, Nebraska. Restrained by several men, a soldier ran him through with a bayonet. Carried into a nearby office, Crazy Horse declined a cot. After he bled to death on the floor his parents took his body away and buried him in an undisclosed location near Wounded Knee Creek.

When Otro awakened in the early morning he found himself wondering how long he would live. He believed he was near the age Crazy Horse had been when he was murdered. What he knew for certain was that during the endless expanse of time that had passed before his birth nothing had troubled him, and nothing would trouble him after he died.

angell

The morning after returning from his angling adventure, Norman Angell climbed out of bed an hour earlier than usual. Still groggy, he pulled on slacks and buttoned up a dress shirt, then breakfasted on two buttered Asiago bagels and three cups of weak black coffee. As he ate he silently cursed his housekeeper, who apparently had ineptly prepared the coffee machine. But he finished the substandard brew to the last swallow and both bagels to the last crumb. He'd developed a powerful hatred of waste, and his secret aspiration was to leave as little as possible behind him when he died.

His frugality extended to the most mundane of life's functions. That morning, in front of the bathroom mirror, he found himself hoping that when he brushed his teeth and applied after-shave lotion for the last time in his life, the toothpaste tube and green glass lotion bottle would be, if not empty, very nearly so.

He rode an empty elevator twenty-three floors down to the street, walked half a block to Starbucks, and took a small corner table to himself. Fifty-two seconds after ordering a double-caffeinated grande – he counted the time off in his head – a sullen young waitress delivered a steaming green mug.

Counting on caffeine to neutralize his hangover, Angell took a deep swallow. At this hour Starbucks was less than half full. All the customers appeared to be businessmen and women. By the time Angell drained his mug his head felt better. From Starbucks it was less than a block to EAIB (Enjoyment At Its Best) Headquarters, where he occupied a spacious office set between a cafeteria and a conference room on the 32nd floor. As planned, he reached the office more than half an hour before his first scheduled meeting. He knew precisely how the meeting would go. Though much of the company's work was done remotely, EAIB's old-fashioned CEO professed the belief that collegial contact solidified companionship and therefore led to better business, so eight executives would sit at a synthetic rosewood table drinking ersatz coffee subtly flavored with organic mint, and talk, and joke, and argue without malice. Should they, in their upcoming sex doll promotions, emphasize humor, science or romance? Or all three? After fifteen or twenty minutes, when the previous month's sales figures were revealed, attendees would congratulate each other for the profits the corporation had reaped. An agreement would be reached on when to meet again.

But now, with some precious time all to himself, Angell took the slender leather-bound book his great-great-grandfather had written from a locked desk drawer.

He sat in one of the three comfortably upholstered chairs facing his desk and reread his favorite chapter, beginning with a description of a mountain stream on an early morning in spring when the only sounds were birdsong and clean, cold water rushing over a boulder-strewn, gravel-bottomed riffle where many large trout held, nosing into the current.

He read about stoneflies hatching and floating downstream soon after first light with the trout rising to intercept them, so many fish feeding that the rings formed on the surface as they swallowed the big, clumsy insects made it look as though rain had begun to fall; about casting an imitation stonefly and hooking wild fish, one after another; about a huge rainbow jumping high after the hook had been set and, for an instant, hanging in the clean air before crashing down, its broad side slamming water with a reverberating splat; about the trout's powerful downstream run through a narrow channel into a deep pool; about landing the fish and admiring its rose-colored lateral line and flashing silver sides through the landing net's wet meshes; about slipping the hook from the undershot jaw and releasing the fish, and watching it right itself, and then hold steady against the current before swimming away, free again, vanishing into deep, dark water.

Angell closed the book gently and locked it into its drawer. Day by day, the world was inexorably deteriorating. Responsible individuals acting independently occasionally managed to slow the process, but there never were or would be enough of them to reverse the decline. Governments, always inept, never acted quickly enough. Understanding all this, Angell wondered why he should want a wife or children, but he couldn't help himself. No matter what, he did.

On the first evening home from his escape he'd dined on wild trout instead of the tainted flesh of a tortured animal killed in a slaughterhouse. He envied his great-great grandfather. He envied trout.

otro

The day after his return from Bereavement Creek Otro drove his old Bronco to Mini's Tavern and, as he'd expected, was the only customer there at mid-day. He ordered a bottle of his favorite beer, Negra Modelo.

Mini's much loved pastime was drawing ink and charcoal portraits, and Otro told her that the man he'd taken fishing to Bereavement Creek, whose face was an archetypical illustration of tragically suppressed grief, would make a worthy subject for her. Mini told Otro about a controversy that had flared up while he was gone. Sheriff Zouch had decided to run for congress and some of the people she and Otro knew were wondering whether it might be possible to somehow sabotage his campaign.

When Otro left Mini's and pulled out of the lot onto the road a member of an urban motorcycle gang, the White Lightnings, sped around a bend on his antique Harley Davidson. After swerving to avoid a collision he came to a quick stop on the roadside ahead. As Otro drove by him the bearded, black-helmeted biker shook a clenched black-gloved fist and screamed: *"Halfbreed! Misfit!"*

Otro made no sign he'd seen or heard the man.

Seconds later the White Lightning caught up with Otro and rode alongside him, screaming over the roar of the Harley from three feet away through the open Bronco window: *"Go back where you came from, half-breed! Mongrel! Motherfucker!"* As the cycle surged away Otro glimpsed a bloated white face encased in the black helmet.

➤◄

The next day Otro took an early morning run. He passed the fire-scarred debris that not long ago had been a wealthy man's country house, then climbed the steep hill beyond and crossed a dam, circled Deadhead Lake, and followed a narrow woodland trail to where it ended at a fetid pond of water next to the long-abandoned saw-mill across the road from Mini's. He walked through a grove of pines into a small clearing to urinate, and there was yesterday's White Lightning, lying dead, close beside a barbed wire fence. Today he wore neither helmet nor gloves. Facedown, his head was twisted sideways, with one leather-jacketed arm draped over the lowest strand of wire. The eye Otro could see was open and bloodshot. A pink scar crossed the white bald spot on the dead man's head. Otro turned away to urinate and then made his way back through the pines to the road. As he stepped out of the trees a muddy van driven by a red-haired woman passed by. Mini's hadn't opened yet so he ran home.

➤·◄

The next afternoon Otro was driving toward home from a distant lake he'd checked out as a probable destination for an Alabama angler booked to fish with him. The Alabaman's goal was to become the first bass fisherman in history to land a verified ten-pound largemouth in every state, and this was state number forty-seven on his list. He had agreed in writing to Otro's stipulations: to use top-water plugs only in order to avoid impaling a bait hook in a fish's stomach; to release all bass weighing less than ten pounds; to quit fishing after a ten-pounder had been landed.

Halfway home Otro approached a hitchhiker standing next to an ancient pickup truck with its hood raised. His inclination was to offer aid whenever and wherever he could, so he coasted to a stop just beyond the pickup and then, in the rearview mirror, watched the hitchhiker jogging toward the Bronco - a young man wearing a soiled white t-shirt tucked into baggy pants with a backpack slung by a single strap over his right shoulder.

"Grassy ass," the hitchhiker said. "Oops. Guess I meant gracias."

"Por nada," Otro answered. "Subir en. Climb in."

"Spurmeister's the name. Ain't exactly Spanish, is it? What's yours?"

"Otro."

"Otro?"

"Otro."

"First or last?"

"Both."

"Well, like, whatever. Old beater truck broke down." Spurmeister settled into the passenger seat and dropped his backpack onto the floor between his legs. The pack's top flap hung open, exposing what Otro recognized as heroin bricks tightly wrapped in blue plastic. He started down the road.

"Hey," Spurmeister said. "You know who Zouch is, right? The Sheriff, right?"

"I know who he is."

"He got a murder on his hands. You heard about it yet?"

"No."

"Some big shot from the city got shot. Somebody found the stiff this morning. Waitin' on the road back there I got the news on my phone. Me, I got no use for

Zouch. Fuck 'im's what I say. Hey, man, what are you, anyway? A Indian or a Mexican or what?"

Otro didn't answer.

"Well then look at me, weirdo."

Otro looked and saw a handgun pointed at him.

"You want somebody to find you dead, weirdo? This pistol right here's the latest model, almost. Just keep on drivin'. All I need's a ride. Got it? If you don't got it, you're gonna get it. Hey. Last week some punk in Omaha gunned down twelve people in a lottery ticket line in ten secionds flat with the same weapon I got right here in my hand. Exact same *kind* of weapon's what I mean. Drive around the limit, weirdo. Kind of slow makes me feel peaceful. Know what I mean? What's the limit in these parts? Fifty-five?"

"That's right."

"I figure you for some kind of beaner, or some kind of half-breed. Or maybe even some rag-head fig-eater."

On the right hand shoulder down the road Otro saw a dead fork-horn buck that had likely been struck and killed in the night. The deer lay on its side, stiff legs pointed toward the road. Smears of dried blood underneath the carcass showed black in the hazy morning light.

"One more dumb-ass road-kill," Spurmeister said. "Don't they ever learn? Guess not! Dumb asses!"

"Animals are superior to people," Otro said. "Not the domesticated species people ruin through breeding or training, or the livestock people slaughter to eat. Wild animals live the way they were meant to live where nature put them. Their major advantage over all of us is that they have no way of knowing that they won't exist exactly as they are forever."

"You are damn sure one spaced-out motherfuckin' weirdo!"

Beyond the dead buck they rounded a curve and entered a forest where tall Douglas firs along both sides of the narrow road formed a shaded tunnel. A pickup truck loaded with hay bales came at them the other way and rushed by. Otro glimpsed the driver - an old white-haired farmer wearing overalls.

"You crazy for real, weirdo? Ready for the fuckin' nut house?"

"No," Otro said. "But you might be."

"Yeah, well, I figure you are, dude." Spurmeister laughed. Then he said, "In maybe a mile you'll hit a old dirt road. See that fuckin' bend way up there ahead?"

"I see it."

"Right after that bend there."

Otro slowed as they rounded the bend.

"See that snag, that humungous fuckin' dead fir?"

"Yes."

"Drop me off right past that. You're a weird-ass nut from who knows where but you did me a favor picking me up. 'Preciate it."

Spurmeister tucked his pistol underneath his waistband and hopped out of the Bronco, lifted his backpack out, slid both arms through the straps and hoisted it onto his shoulders. The rutted, overgrown logging road led straight back through second-growth firs as far as Otro could see.

"Adios, weirdo," Spurmeister said with a smile. "Grassy ass," he called back over his shoulder as he walked away.

>·◄

Otro always wanted to learn as much as he could about potential enemies. He watched Spurmeister walk down the logging road for a minute or more without looking back. Then Otro drove around another bend, parked in a roadside clearing, and ran back at a quick pace the way he'd come. When he reached the logging road he followed its course. He passed a small creek where the water looked and smelled clean and stopped to drink his fill. Soon after that he sighted Spurmeister striding along, leaning forward, head down, hands gripping the backpack straps. Otro kept to the cover of trees and followed until Spurmeister stopped and cupped his hands around his mouth and yelled, "Hey dudes! It's me!"

"We know who it is, Spurm," came an answer. "Where the fuck you been, asshole?"

Sheltered by sword ferns, Otro saw two men standing together at a meadow's edge, one leaning on a shovel, the other on a pick. A muddy all-terrain van was parked directly behind them. Then he saw a third man sitting cross-legged on the ground near the van, his back against a weathered log. The pick and shovel men wore work pants, white t-shirts and wide-brimmed straw hats. The one on the ground, wearing faded jeans and a red t-shirt, was missing his left arm. The left t-shirt sleeve had been cut off at the shoulder and the pink stump of the arm protruded through the opening. Then Otro saw a corpse flat on its back, partially concealed by a thick patch of star thistle.

Spurmeister stopped to face the pick and shovel men. "Tough fuckin' morning," he said. "Had to get around a dried out mudslide. Almost turned my old man's piece of shit truck over. A few miles after that the fucker broke down. Tranny I guess. Got me a lift from a whacked out weirdo. Dropped me off back on the highway."

"Just so you have the product."

"Yeah I do!" Spurmeister slipped out of the straps, lowered his backpack to the ground and pulled back the top flap. "Right here!"

When Otro moved a few feet closer he saw the freshly dug grave behind the corpse. The dead young man wore a bright yellow t-shirt, short pants and scuffed leather boots, and his narrow face was white as the belly of a trout, the eyes closed, mouth wide open. Two flies landed on the pale skin and walked across the smooth forehead and flew away and quickly returned.

The man with the pick leaned over to take a long look into the backpack and finally nodded his head. "Okay, Spurm," he said. "You're cool. All we got left is to plant Hatch."

"Who killed ol' Hatch?"

"I did," the one-armed man answered.

"How come?"

""Cause we got verified word he cut a deal with the sheriff."

"Zouch?"

"Zouch."

"Why would he cut a deal with that motherfucker?"

"When Hatch delivered our payoff he talked to Zouch about our routes and delivery times. Zouch handed back the payoff in exchange for the info. Zouch's deputy – some moron named Dipple - told me about it. Dipple saw it happen. I found the cash in Hatch's back pocket right after I drilled him."

"I thought Hatch was cool," Spurmeister said.

"You ready to help dig?"

"I guess."

"Well then do it, Spurm. Like now."

Spurmeister walked over to place his pistol on top of the weathered log and walked back scratching his head. The man he took the pick from spat a stream of tobacco juice that made a long brown stain on Hatch's t-shirt.

Otro watched the men dig the grave and listened to them talk.

"It's a fucking surprise to me," Spurmeister said. "I figured Hatch was a good man. How deep's this need to be?"

"Not too deep," the one-armed man said. "Nobody cares about stiffs planted in the boondocks. I mean there's stiffs all over the place out here. No names, no coffins, no nothing. You heard about Leopold yet?"

"What about him?"

"He was on vacation in Hawaii. On Kauai. They got hit with two feet of rain in one day."

"Yeah, I heard about that."

"Dudes drowned all over the place. Dudettes too. Is it dudesses or dudettes? Anyway that's where Leopold was, Kauai."

Spurmeister stepped out of the shallow grave and the one with the shovel stepped in to toss clods of earth back over his shoulder.

For half an hour Otro watched the men take turns with the pick and shovel, making small talk as they worked. The apparent leader, the amputee, took a brief one-armed turn with the pick. The others called him "Lefty."

"Fuck it," Lefty finally said. "It's deep enough."

The four men carried Hatch by his arms and legs, Lefty taking an ankle with his remaining hand. Hatch landed in his grave with a loud thump.

Running through the trees back to his Bronco Otro remembered the time he'd worked in Chicago as a medical technician. Because he was in that city he read an early 20th century novel set there. The protagonist was an Irish boy named Studs who rationalized the futile work he did by concluding that his job was where his pork chops came from. Apparently Hatch had been shot dead for wanting more than his fair share of pork chops. Wherever they came from, or wherever they lived, most people wanted all the pork chops they could get.

lefty

Lefty's proper name was Douglas Cooke. He could barely remember his mother, an ophthalmologist, who at age
forty dropped dead of a heart attack rushing across a
busy crosswalk to beat a yellow llight on her way to her
office. Douglas grew up in Cambridge, Massachusetts
with his father, a highly regarded professor of physics
at Harvard University. During Doug's sophomore year
at Boston University Professor Cooke resigned his Harvard appointment to join a corporation that specialized
in earth-to-space weaponry, a position that more than
doubled his already more than ample salary. Doug decided that his father's egocentricity might be forgivable,
but not his breach of ethics.

Sitting after dinner in their dining room, a servant
having cleared the table, a cello concerto playing quietly, Doug had done his best to defend arguments com-
mon among his peers to his father - old arguments with
updated details. By lavishly funding what government
functionaries euphemistically called "national defense,"
modern weaponry slaughtered tens of thousands of innocent civilians per year, rarely if ever for acceptable motives. The money squandered on lethal weapons could
be gainfully spent on efforts to preserve human life – all
life - on planet earth. Doug spoke his mind respectfully,
but, when he finished, his father shook his bald head in
wonderment, laughed in his face, and walked out of the
room.

Doug dropped out of Boston University the next day and nine days after that left home amicably. His father had opened a bank account in his name. "There's more than enough money in it for you to do something," he said, "but not enough for you to do nothing. I don't have exceptionally high hopes for you, but I do wish you luck. You know I'll be here if and when you need me." Along with the bank account he gifted his son with a heavy-duty rebuilt van complete with kitchen, bathroom and sleeping quarters.

Like so many tens of millions of Americans before him, Doug headed west. He traveled on secondary roads whenever possible all the way to Portland, Oregon, 3,211 miles away. He observed the towns and countryside, listened to music and podcasts through the days, ate simple meals, slept comfortably at night, and did his best to appreciate the first true freedom he'd ever experienced. The downside of what he saw were drought-ravaged and flooded farmland, polluted rivers and lakes, barren prairies and scorched forests. In one rural town there were melted cars and ash heaps that had been houses.

There were pleasant sights too – green forests, deserts, rivers and lakes, occasional birds and animals. For the first time in his life Doug saw Huck Finn's Mississippi River. After the Great Plains came the snowcapped Rocky Mountains where the van withstood hail storms and flooded roads. Winds across the flats of Wyoming exceeded 70 miles per hour. In Idaho mudslides had closed so many roads that the van, in its computerized wisdom, routed him across the wastelands of Nevada, and then northward through the Steens Mountains in southeastern Oregon.

Biding his time in Portland, living in the van, thinking, making chance contacts, trying to decide what he might do with his immediate future, Doug eventually fell in with politically active young people and soon joined them in protest demonstrations against manifestations of the ubiquitous cruelty and greed exhibited by too many people in power. During a Saturday afternoon march through downtown, objecting to a proposed bill that would inevitably lead to students paying more and professors earning less, a counter-demonstrator threw a homemade grenade from a third floor window into a crowd of marchers. Two young men and a young woman marching behind Doug died instantly. Doug's left arm, mutilated by shrapnel, had to be amputated.

By the time Doug left the hospital six days after the amputation, having thought it over carefully, he made up his spiteful mind to do something comparable to what his father had done. He'd read extensively about drug cartels and how they were organized and operated, and he saw himself functioning as a successful businessman, a prosperous middleman, buying from carefully chosen producers and selling to carefully screened distributors. He'd call himself Lefty and, once well established, he'd get his measure of revenge by letting his father know the choice he'd made.

otro

Late in the afternoon the day after Hatch was buried Sheriff Zouch arrived at Otro's dwelling to accuse him of murder. Otro courteously gave him permission to search the premises. Hoping for a firearm, all Zouch found were hunting bows and knives. "We'll nail you!" he said. "*I* will! I'm on this case hard! You figure me for dumb? Well I ain't! *You're* the dumbbell – dumpin' the innocent victim you shot right across the road from your hangout! You think that lawyer friend you got can save you? I know all about that Jew! No fuckin' way, Jose. I'll be picking you up tomorrow morning. I'm givin' you some time to think! You know how to think? How to figure out you better confess? Tomorrow morning then! Somebody'll be watchin' you from now till then! Ten o'clock! Be here!"

Zouch, standing in the middle of the driveway, legs spread, thumbs hooked over his black leather belt, glowered at Otro through narrowed eyes. "All you are's a misfit, a nobody!" When he lifted a big white hand to scratch his head, Otro turned and started up the driveway. "I'll nail you! I been checkin' it all out! You never should've come to these parts an' you been here way too long already! Hear me, misfit?"

Otro didn't answer.

"Gloria paid you off! His wife did! Gloria! Am I right?"

Otro was halfway up his front steps by the time he heard Zouch drive away. He knew that years ago in the city where he'd worked Zouch had been dispatched with other cops to help control a wild downtown melee. He ended up swinging his baton at a tattooed boy wrapped in a green flag but the boy ducked and Zouch's baton fractured the skull of a teenage girl. She happened to be a wealthy man's daughter and two days later she died. That was how Zouch ended up exiled to the boondocks.

Zouch's downfall had happened the same year Otro built his cabin with logs harvested from the thirty acres of land he'd purchased with his savings. The cabin sat on the gentle slope of a grassy hill at the edge of a clearing in a river valley. He had one fair-sized room containing a single bed, a homemade table with four wooden chairs, and a pinewood trunk that held both kitchen utensils and clothing. In the middle of the room was a Schrader woodstove that served for cooking and provided winter heat. A door to the left of the bed led to a bathroom, and a door to the right led to a storage closet. Outside the front door was a narrow deck, and beyond that a fenced pasture for Otro's appaloosa stallion, Eagle. At the pasture's bottom edge next to the split-rail fence were a shelter for Eagle, a smokehouse and a woodshed. Otro smoked wild meat with apple wood from a long-abandoned orchard eight miles up the creek. He piped his water from a spring near the top of the hill. It was all he wanted and all he'd ever need.

Sitting on the deck with his morning coffee, Otro liked to watch Eagle graze. For a day or two after a storm had cleared the air he could see distant mountain ranges. He liked the mountains best on infrequent winter days when sunlight shone on new-fallen snow. Throughout the year small flocks of ducks and geese passed overhead and sometimes a hawk or turkey vulture circled high in a summer sky. On early mornings a deer or two might emerge from the trees to feed at the edge of a clearing. Sometimes after darkness fell Otro sat on the deck with a bottle of beer or a shot of tequila. On nights when the air was clear he watched stars along with satellites and space junk crossing the sky. Sometimes the dead he'd loved came to vivid life in his mind. Now he had friends and a woman he loved. He felt himself luckier than most.

zouch

Joseph Zouch didn't want to think about her but he couldn't help himself. It was two months short of twenty years since he had last seen Josephina Gomez in the flesh, but she lingered in his mind as clearly as if it had been twenty days. All that time ago they both had been eighteen-year-old high school seniors. Zouch, a nose guard, captained a championship football team and gloried in his reputation as a player who hit as hard as any defensive high school lineman in the state. He also carried the reputation of a merciless street fighter who beat rivals senseless and bloody.

Back then two things bothered Zouch. The first was that his single mother, Cassidy Zouch, operated an escort service that served political leaders and wealthy businessmen who passed through town. The plain-spoken truth was that his mother was a female pimp who sold high-priced whores to rich men. The second troublesome issue was the fact that he had no way of knowing who his biological father was, because his mother had been inseminated at a sperm bank. A large, copper-framed photo prominently displayed in her townhouse living room showed her posed on a white divan with an exuberant smile on her face, cradling the infant Joseph with her right arm while holding an over-sized test tube toward the camera in her left hand. In the background were six tall coconut palms with a placid blue sea behind them. What his mother called the "family portrait" enraged Zouch. It never occurred to him that his mom might have a sense of humor.

Josephina Gomez, daughter of a Hispanic father and blond mother from Gothenburg, Sweden, was an above average student and the loveliest young woman at Ronald Reagan High School. The physical results of her disparate genes were stunning, and no one was surprised when the student body elected her homecoming queen. Zouch became homecoming king, having threatened the nerdish boy in charge of tabulating ballots with a brutal beating if he didn't win the election.

Two weeks after the state championship football game Zouch escorted Josephina to the celebratory prom. When he picked her up wearing a stylish rented tuxedo she met him at the door of her home in a white satin gown. She wore no makeup, because she needed none. Her bright smile and blue eyes glowed with apparent pleasure, and on one side of the white gown black hair fell in glossy waves to her narrow waist. In her high heels she was nearly as tall as Zouch.

When they danced together Zouch felt clumsy, something he'd never experienced on a football field, and when they talked as they danced, or while sitting at a table between dances, he was nervous nearly to the point of panic. Gawking at her beauty, his hands shook and he stammered and blushed.

For some enigmatic reason Zouch hadn't understood either at the time or through all the years since then, Josephina liked him. Toward the end of the evening, when the lights were dimmed and slow retro music played, she pressed herself tightly against him. Luckily, before the prom, thanks to a teammate's suggestion, Zouch had securely taped his penis to his leg so as not to embarrass himself with an untimely hard-on.

As he drove Josephina home she told him of her future plans. She'd recently won a scholarship to Brown University with plans to become a pre-med major. "When I finally become a pediatrician," she said, "I want to serve the poor."

"We kind of got the same first names," was all Zouch could think of in reply. He couldn't work up sufficient nerve to try to kiss Josephina goodnight. "'Night," he mumbled, looking at the toes of his shoes. "Thanks," he added in a whisper.

Standing at the doorway of her house in moonlight, she kissed him. Hands resting on his shoulders, she pressed against him hard as she thrust her tongue into his mouth. The tape held. After a few seconds her hands were gone and she turned away. "I like you very much, Joseph," she said, and then he heard the door close.

Standing alone, still staring at the toes of his polished black shoes, Zouch could taste the sugary lemonade Josephina had drunk at the prom.

Throughout the rest of the school year he had never been able to work up enough courage to speak to her again. He admired her from a distance, longed for her, dreamt of her often, and soon after graduation she was gone.

After the prom Zouch centered his future hopes on football, but not a single major college offered him a scholarship. A few coaches watched his video highlights, and one of them complimented his aggressive play, but explained that at 210 pounds he wasn't nearly big enough to succeed as a defensive lineman at the Division 1 level.

Zouch remained certain that toughness was more important than thirty or forty extra pounds of flesh. But when he contacted coaches at smaller schools, one after another, he suffered the same result. He wasn't considered big enough even for them. Finally, a month before fall practice was scheduled to begin, he convinced the head coach of a small state school desperate for defensive linemen to give him a tryout.

Zouch promised himself that once he won his scholarship he would reestablish contact with Josephina at Brown University, wherever it was. He had a friend who could write a letter for him to sign, a letter filled with love. But after two weeks of hard workouts, the coach, a wheezing old man, called Zouch into his office and cut him. "You tried," he said in a kindly voice from behind his littered desk. "You tried hard, and I respect that. You're a strong boy and you keep yourself in shape. I respect that too. Believe me, I do. I mean, look at me. I'm a friggin wreck. But the truth of the matter at hand is, this level of football's not in the cards for you. I wish you well, son."

Zouch had no answer, and he wouldn't allow himself to cry in front of the old coach, but he cried when he turned his back and slammed the door behind him, thinking of Josephina.

His pimp mother's enterprise had expanded to neighboring states and then overseas, so she could easily have paid his way to any college that would take him, but Zouch wanted no part of what people called higher education. For three years after high school he worked at various menial jobs while living in his mother's beachside vacation home. When he saw himself gaining weight in the wrong places he began lifting barbells and running on a treadmill at a gym, where he came to know a police sergeant who also worked out there. One day when they were on adjoining treadmills the sergeant told Zouch that the city needed young cops in good physical shape and that, if interested, he should apply.

"We need tough young studs to keep the rabble-rousers in line," the sergeant explained. "There's more fucking druggies and hoodlums out there all the time. Every color, shape and size, *every* goddamn where. Too many scumbags!"

Zouch applied at City Hall the next day. He passed a background check, a psychological exam, a physical exam – which seemed laughably easy - and became a cop. He was proud to join the force, to have a respectable occupation. Finally he'd succeeded at something and gained his independence. As blind luck would have it, two weeks after he moved into his own downtown apartment, the vacation home he'd been living in, perched high on a cliff, with his mother in it, tumbled into a churning sea during a violent storm.

Zouch collected insurance money, hired a financial adviser recommended by an uncle to invest his inheritance, and celebrated by tossing the "family portrait" into a dumpster. Even though wealthy, he stayed on the police force because he thoroughly enjoyed the work. What he liked most were opportunities to beat people soundly in what could pass for the line of duty.

otro

Sitting on his deck, nursing a tequila, Otro wondered what Zouch had in mind. As daylight faded two nighthawks appeared over Eagle's pasture. Otro watched them swoop and bank gracefully on long, pointed wings as they fed on insects. At the far end of the pasture a half-grown cinnamon-colored bear walked out of the trees to drink at the creek, then raised himself on hind paws and stood gazing at Eagle. When the stallion looked back the bear dropped to all fours and returned to the shelter of trees. Soon a nearly full moon appeared, followed by dim, barely discernible stars in the eastern sky. Otro smelled rain and calculated it would take no more than two hours for the storm to arrive. He decided to run to Mini's Tavern, where members of his tribe would be. At a relaxed pace he covered the six miles in thirty-eight minutes.

"Otro!" said Gold when he walked in. "Welcome back!"

"Otro!" said Sand.

"Otro!" said Mini.

"Mini!" Otro answered. "Sand! Gold!"

The room held five round varnished pinewood tables that circled a fire pit where three charred logs lay on a gray bed of ashes. Gold, Sand and Mini were at the table nearest the fire pit. All four log walls were bare except for a lineup of liquor bottles on a single wooden shelf behind the bar. A cooler sat on the floor below the liquor shelf and Mini sat on a stool next to the cooler. With beer bottles beside them and a chess board between them, Gold and Sand sat facing one another.

There was no sign out front, so few people knew the tavern existed. Mini ran the place as what amounted to a private club, and only her friends were accepted as members, with occasional exceptions made for backpackers and truck drivers. The absentee owner, who lived in a distant city, used the so-called business as a tax write-off, and the amount of money the place lost was irrelevant. Mini charged her friends a dime for a bottle of beer and fifteen cents for a shot of quality tequila. Two or three days a week she cooked, and a decent lunch or dinner cost fifty cents.

"Cerveza por favor," Otro told her.

"Oscuro?"

"Por supuesto."

Mini had smooth brown skin, straight shoulder-length black hair and a slim though muscular body. She thought of herself as a strictly amateur artist and had never shown her work to anyone except Otro's lady-friend Loot. She usually wore a smile and laughed often and claimed that drawing in ink and charcoal made her happy and kept her that way. She reached into the cooler and brought out a water-beaded brown bottle of Negra Modelo. The color of the bottle nearly matched her skin. Foam spilled over the top when she opened the bottle, and after handing it to Otro she wiped her hands dry on her sweatshirt. "One thin dime," she said to him with a smile.

"I never carry that much cash," Otro said. "You'll have to put it on my bill."

She stopped smiling. "Zouch was here," she said.

"When?"

"Late afternoon."

"He told us he'd come from your place," Gold said. "That he'd be picking you up again tomorrow morning to take you in for what he called 'serious questioning.' I gave him some pro bono legal counsel. I robustly advised him not to overdo it."

"What did he want here?"

"Questioned us," Sand said. "About you. Of course we didn't tell him anything."

Otro sat leaning back on a wooden chair with one front leg missing. Fewer than half the pieces remained on the chess board, and the blacks that belonged to Gold outnumbered the whites two to one.

Gold was middle-aged with curly grey hair, a clean-shaved face, brown skin, bright blue eyes and a massive upper body. His short legs were malformed due to an early childhood traffic accident. When he understood what had happened to him, and what it meant, he decided to develop his torso to serve as what he called reparations. On a stifling summer afternoon alongside the road in front of the tavern Otro had watched him take a pickup truck's back bumper in his hands and lift the vehicle off the ground to hold it high enough and long enough for the owner to change a tire.

Gold swallowed beer and moved a bishop on the chessboard. "Check," he said to Sand.

Sand stared at the board.

"There's one decent defensive move you can make," Gold said.

"How many lousy defensive moves can I make?"

Gold briefly studied the board. "Eleven," he said. "No, twelve." He drank beer and held his bottle out over the table. "Prost," he said.

"Das Bier schmeckt," Otro said, and clinked his bottle against Gold's.

"Zouch told us something," Gold said. "Something I know he knew we'd tell you."

"What?"

"That a woman saw you coming out of the trees the morning before they found O'brien's body. She knew who you were and told Zouch about it when she learned about the dead man."

"Who found the body?"

"Zouch didn't say."

"The dead man was named O'brien?"

"Yes."

"Why would Zouch want you to tell me about the woman who saw me?"

"So you'd know he has a witness. I told him I'd be handling your defense if a formal legal defense becomes necessary."

"What did he say to that?"

"Not a word. He's a moron, not quite an imbecile, so he understands that I still have connections. No government cares much about us way out here and they won't send anybody to straighten out a mess unless they absolutely have to. But I can arrange things so that they have to, and I'm fairly sure even Zouch understands that."

Sand finally moved a knight.

"You don't want to move there," Gold said.

Sand looked hard at the board. "Yes I do," he finally answered.

"For certain?"

"Yes."

Gold moved a rook the length of the board. "Checkmate," he said. "Take it back and try another move."

"Thanks, but no thanks," Sand said. "I've had enough."

Gold leaned back in his chair and looked at Otro. "Zouch told me some things about O'brien," he said. "He was a very wealthy businessman, a business owner, with connections of his own. That's one reason Zouch has to take his death somewhat seriously. The fact is Zouch has an election coming up. Did you know that? He's running for congress. He wants to represent our hayseed shit-kicker right-wing district back in Washington. But in any case you should've reported finding the body. I know you didn't kill the man, but why didn't you tell somebody about it? That was a mistake."

"If this place had been open that morning I'd have come in and told Mini. By the time I reached home I'd decided not to get involved with the law."

"Understandable," Sand said.

Sand was a homely man a foot taller than Gold, so skinny he looked to be malnourished. In his patched and faded jeans and tie-dyed t-shirt, with his long grey hair tied into a ponytail, he looked like a starving refugee hippy from the 1960s. He had been a cardiothoracic surgeon and refused to say a word about why he'd finally decided on an extremely alternative life.

"O'brien was shot in the chest," Mini said. "Twice. Zouch told us that."

"I didn't see any blood when I found him."

"Zouch says he was killed someplace else and dumped where he was found afterwards," Gold said. "Dumped by you."

o'brien

His high fashion male clothing enterprise had made Patrick O'brien rich enough to possess a 10,000 square foot mid-city penthouse and two extravagant vacation homes, one on 72 groomed acres that included a man-made lake, the other in an alpine meadow with easy access to downhill skiing on manufactured snow. Despite his property holdings and various accoutrements - including a 200-foot yacht anchored off southern California, and a private aircraft staffed with a permanent crew - his Harley Davidson Hog secretly became his most prized possession.

Before the Harley purchase, O'brien had suffered through several years of sporadic sexual impotence. The most costly treatments he could find didn't help, and he attributed his malfunction to his bleak home life.

After a calculated courtship he had succeeded in marrying an attractive red-haired Irish woman, with the express intent of making use of her wealthy family's international connections, thereby enabling his corporation to exploit cheap foreign labor and eventually – soon enough - more than double its sales and profit margin.

But trouble began within weeks of the Dublin, Ireland wedding, when Kelly Anne came to clearly understand her husband's motives. She immediately dedicated herself to making his life wretched. Wherever the two of them were on earth, in public places she conspicuously ignored him, and in private she verbally abused him, usually with traditional Irish insults. On rare occasions when he tried to initiate sex, she often called him a "lick-arse gobshite without bullocks." When she took peri-odic male and female lovers, instead of trying to hide her trysts, she made certain he learned about them, in graphic detail.

O'brien, sensitive to the reputation Irishmen had for drinking too much, had always kept his alcohol con-sumption under strict control. He would take a sociable drink or two at a business lunch or dinner, and that was it. But soon after Kelly Anne turned against him, he be-gan drinking at home too, first beer or wine with dinner, then mixed drinks with dinner, and finally straight Irish whiskey, before, during and after dinner.

Kelly Anne bore two children, a son and a daugh-ter, and when her husband suggested they be tested to authenticate his paternity, she refused. "There's a chance they're yours," she told him. "Maybe not much of a chance, but who the fuck knows, one of them might be. But why would you want to risk ruining things for your-self with the truth, you hopeless dryshite?"

By ages five and seven, the children, Colleen and Connor, urged by their mother, had learned to insult their father to his face. Finally, at the dinner table, when a smirking Connor commented that the bald spot on Daddy's head was growing by the day, O'brien back-handed him hard enough to knock two teeth out. He tried to convince Kelly Anne that they might be baby teeth, so it really didn't matter. But three nights later, when her husband passed out after too much whiskey, Kelly Anne drained the bottle and smashed the empty against the bald spot on his skull, opening a gash that took a dozen stitches and left a nasty pink scar.

For years O'brien had been both curious and envious about the White Lightnings, a motorcycle gang of men who rode Harleys to invade and harass the world's minorities and useless nobodies, and, when opportunities presented themselves, engage in one-sided brawls. Gang members and their devotees posted social media commentary and video footage that was seen by millions, including O'brien. Individual gang members were never identified by name but were always described as highly successful men whose allegedly unlawful activities complemented their stressful lives, even fulfilled them. Though on rare occasions police arrested a White Lightning or two and locked them up, it was strictly for show. Thanks to their bank accounts and their lawyers, the short-term prisoners were always treated well and set free within a matter of hours. Brief jail time not only didn't shame White Lightnings, it triggered macho pride.

O'brien bought the glistening black restored Harley from an antique dealer who swore that the bike had been used in the 1953 Marlon Brando movie, "The Wild One." As soon as O'brien learned to ride the machine with confidence he joined the gang. They were delighted to have him. On his first day members told him he was a natural, that he fit their mold perfectly. Before three months had passed he became something of a leader. Roaming the roads on his Harley, O'brien could wear whatever he wanted, could curse freely and raise hell, and, most importantly, could impose his will on the world's hopeless losers. Riding his Harley into action with other White Lightnings he felt intensely alive, a bona fide man. When he rode alone, looking for whatever entertainment or hassle he might find, he felt like more than a man. He temporarily became what he hadn't been since his teenage years, a rough-and-tumble stud. After every excursion, back home in his private bedroom, naked except for his cycling helmet, he took advantage of his black market sex doll, a blond programmed with a heavy German accent that had been modeled after Lilly Von Shtupp, a character in the 20th century satirical cowboy movie, "Blazing Saddles."

As a White Lightning life was well worth living again.

alejandro

After his chess loss to Gold Sand walked to the bar and came back to place a shiny Koa wood box on the table. He opened the brass-hinged lid and carefully placed each chess piece into its felt-lined niche.

"Is there a chance Zouch could win his congressional election?" Otro asked the table.

"It's possible," Gold said. "If he does he'll suck in graft from every direction. If he wasn't running he wouldn't much care about O'brien's murder. But convicting you would definitely improve his chances."

"Rumors have it Zouch is wealthy," Otro said.

"The rumors are true. He inherited a lot of money. Money's not really what he's after. He's after what his underdeveloped and insecure mind perceives as power."

"Richtig," Otro said. "Danke fur Ihre Hilfe."

"Bitte," Gold answered.

Sand carried the black box back to the bar and handed it over to Mini.

Back at the table Sand and Gold began discussing art. Gold loved Van Gogh and Sand favored Picasso, but they never argued about their preferences. Instead, they did their best to define each artist's unique strengths. A car stopped out front while Gold was explaining the most important differences between neo and post-impressionism.

Seconds later Alejandro came through the door. He worked as a mechanic and visited the tavern only at night. As the door swung shut behind him he bowed to the table and straightened up and smiled.

"Buenos noches!" he said.

"Alejandro!" Otro said.

"Guten Abend!" Gold said.

"Hombre!" Sand said.

"Cerveza?" asked Mini.

"Tequila, por favor."

Alejandro sat next to Sand. He was a tall, handsome man with a thick black mustache, and the threadbare clothes he wore when he wasn't working were, as always, immaculate.

Mini brought his tequila in a tall, slender, blue-tinted shot glass. Leaning over to place the glass on the table, she kissed Alejandro's cheek.

"Gracias," Alejandro said with a nod and a smile.

"Por nada, querido," Mini answered.

"We were talking about Zouch," Gold said.

"Malo," Alejandro said. "Un pendejo grande."

"Un cabron," Sand said.

"Un hijo de puta," Alejandro said.

"Correcto," Mini said. "Si."

➤•➥

Alejandro Alvarez was descended from four generations of mechanics who had worked on motor vehicles up and down the thousand-mile length of Mexico's Baja Peninsula. Some of their repair jobs had become local legends. The people of San Ignacio, a village roughly halfway down the peninsula and halfway between the Pacific Ocean and the Sea of Cortez, still tell strangers what Alejandro's great-grandfather did on a hot summer day.

A farmer was driving his wife, who was anticipating childbirth, southward in a rattletrap truck to the town of La Paz. When the truck broke down a few miles south of San Ignacio the farmer hitched a ride back to the village for help. With a folded tarp and his tools in a gunnysack, the mechanic Alvarez drove the husband back to the disabled truck. As he spread the tarp to begin work a young couple driving home to San Ignacio from Santa Rosalia stopped, the man to offer help, the wife to offer comfort to the farmer and his wife.

With his helper, Alejandro quickly dismantled the truck's engine. When the parts lay exposed he inspected them one by one, cleaned many of them, made adjustments to some, and then reassembled the engine. The truck started at once, the engine ran smoothly, and the farmer's wife reached the La Paz hospital hours before her daughter was born.

As a young man Alejandro had performed a Baja Highway miracle of his own when, several miles north of San Ignacio, he came upon a distraught, elderly gringo couple in a disabled motor-home. The right front wheel had inexplicably locked. Alejandro inspected the wheel and, in his broken English, asked the husband for permission to look through their motor-home to possibly discover a part that would allow him to repair it. With some reluctance – after all, poor Mexicans were believed by many gringos to be likely thieves – the husband finally agreed. Alejandro found the part he could use in a fire extinguisher, quickly mended the wheel, and the couple drove to San Ignacio to spend the night. When word of what Alejandro had done spread to village inhabitants, no one was surprised.

Beginning a few months after his motor-home wheel repair job, Alejandro spent two years working his way north from San Ignacio to America. He knew that he could make more money there and send most of it home. On his way north he mined copper, worked in fields and orchards, installed dry wall in houses, washed dishes, did nighttime janitorial work in office buildings, packaged chickens, and cleaned fish. Now that he had been in the country for three years, he loved his work as a mechanic more than ever. It was necessary labor that the men in his family had always done, and he knew that the ability to do it well was carried in their blood. The other love of Alejandro's life, an even stronger love, a lucky miracle, was Mini.

otro

Another car stopped out front, and this time when the tavern door opened Loot walked in. "Otro!" she said, and then looked in turn at each of the others. "Mini! Alejandro! Sand! Gold!"

Loot, a full-blood Sioux, was an artist and a runner. In a calculated attempt to achieve a small measure of her people's revenge she sold paintings, and she ran because she loved it. She had a lithe athlete's body, green eyes, and thick black hair that fell well below her waist. At Stanford University, where she majored in history and captained the women's cross-country team, she took up painting. Because her paintings now sold for high prices, Otro, as a joke, had given her the pseudo-Indian name Counts Her Loot. Soon he shortened it to Loot, and everyone ended up calling her that.

"Cerveza?" Mini asked.

"Ye`," Loot answered in Sioux.

Otro stood and they kissed. She smelled faintly of turpentine. He carried a chair from another table and placed it next to his.

After Mini brought Loot's beer they all talked.

"We were trying out words and phrases that suitably describe the sheriff," Gold told Loot.

"Repellent," she suggested.

"Que es repellent?" Alejandro asked.

"Disgusting," Loot said. "Repulsive. Like a dead animal rotting on the road on a hot day." She paused. "Or a steaming pile of shit."

"Correcto," Alejandro said. "Mierda."

"Scheisse," Gold said.

Loot took Otro's hand. "Did Zouch give you trouble?"

"All he did was insult me – what I suppose he does to a lot of people."

"What did you do?"

"Not much."

"Are you all right?"

"Yes."

"For sure?"

"He's supposed to be taking me in for questioning tomorrow."

"When?"

"He said at ten o'clock in the morning. But he'll be late."

Distant thunder sounded.

"Rain," Sand said. "And soon."

"Si," Alejandro said. "Lluvia. Mucho."

"I'm having those goddamn transmission problems again," Gold said to Alejandro. "The gears slip and it's noisy in neutral."

As Alejandro and Gold talked, the thunder sounded again, louder.

"No problema," Alejandro said to Gold. "Bring it to me in the morning."

Suddenly, rain hammered the roof.

"Time to go," Otro said.

Loot smiled. "Running home in the rain?"

"Yes."

"I'll drive you instead. We can stand naked out in the rain at your place."

"Ye," Otro said.

"Bueno," Alejandro said. "Perfecto."

Everybody laughed.

Loot drove them through the downpour. At Otro's they stood together on the deck, naked in the hard rain, and after that she stayed the night.

In Otro's dream a bunch of crimson grapes was served to him in a deep stone bowl outside a cave overlooking Mill Creek in what was once northern California's Yahi Indian country. In 1915 a lone Yahi the whites named Ishi – "man" - emerged from the Mill Creek canyon to appear at a farm among the Mount Lassen foothills. The Yahi was housed at the University of California Berkeley and soon died there of tuberculosis. He became known as the last wild Indian in North America, and a scholarly book was written about him. In Otro's dream Ishi offered him the bowl. "Each grape tastes better than the one before," Ishi explained. "When you eat the last grape you'll die. I died and so did all my people before me. Eat the grapes and join us."

Otro ate the grapes one by one and what Ishi had told him was true. The first grape was delicious, and each grape afterwards tasted better than the last. When Otro came to the final grape he held it at arm's length between his thumb and index finger. "Eat," Ishi said. Otro placed the grape back in the bowl and smiled at Ishi, who smiled back.

>•<

Late at night the rain stopped, then shortly before dawn it came down harder than ever. Loot and Otro lay in bed in the dark with his arm under her smooth back and her head pressed against his muscular shoulder, and they talked while they listened to the rain. Because he'd been out of touch during his time with Norman Angell, Otro asked about the wildfire season.

"The worst fires right now are in southwestern Colorado. Thousands of acres burned so far and no containment yet."

"Southwest Colorado burned a few years ago."

"It's burning again."

"Fires and floods," Otro said. "Hurricanes and tornadoes."

"Dead children," Loot said. "That's the worst."

Not long before Otro had taken Angell fishing Loot had told him she was pregnant, a circumstance they hadn't planned for. "What about our child?" he asked her.

"I'm healthy, I feel fine, stronger than ever. Do you want our child?"

"The question is, are we sure we want our child to have to live in the world that's well on its way?"

"Exactly. That's the question."

"Have you talked to Sand?"

"He'll abort if we want," Loot said. "If not he'll help with the delivery. Your wet hair still smells like rain.

"Rain creates pleasant odors."

"One of the best is sagebrush after rain. By the way, I slept with Mini while you were gone. Twice."

"Does Alejandro mind?"

"I don't think he knows yet. Do you mind?"

"No. Why would I? She's a fine woman."

"Yes she is," Loot agreed. "Those portraits she does are simple, deceptive, imaginative, true. They're authentic works of art."

"She should show them to Gold and Sand. They care a lot about art. They never argue about it, but who do you think is the better painter, Picasso or Van Gogh?"

"Trying to decide which of two fine things is best makes no sense. That's why Gold and Sand don't argue. Touch me."

"There?"

"Ye."

gold

The generous present Gold's parents gave him when he graduated from Columbia University was a two-month-long European vacation. The young man spent time in predictable cities: London, Madrid, Munich, Budapest,

Prague, Vienna, Paris, Rome. But unlike most inexperienced travelers, he took no tours and spent as little time as possible with compatriots. Instead, despite his misshapen legs, he limped along city streets from early morning until late at night, covering at least twenty miles per day, and learning more through random observations and experiences than he could have by looking at the attractions travel writers and profiteers suggest people should visit.

Gold barely glimpsed the Eifel Tower at a distance but in his wanderings he recognized street, cafe and restaurant names he remembered from books about the city's early 20th century art and literary scene. He found it enlivening to occupy the same spaces once inhabited by Vincent Van Gogh, Pablo Picasso, Alberto Giacometti, Marc Chagall, Gertrude Stein, Ernest Hemingway, Scott Fitzgerald, John Paul Sartre, Albert Camus. On a warm summer afternoon he ate a delicious beefsteak tartar at the Café de la Paix on the Place de l'Opera, which appeared in the early Hemingway story "My Old Man." After his meal Gold drank a cognac at the nearby Harry's New York Bar, where Hemingway and Sinclair Lewis had hung out.

Though in his youth he hadn't cared excessively about painters and their work, and had somehow passed by the Louvre without knowing it was there, he idly followed a lovely French girl into the Musee d'Orsay the morning before he departed Paris for Rome. At a discreet distance, he walked behind her into the Vincent Van Gogh room. The instant he saw his first Van

Gogh he forgot about the girl. The reproductions he had seen in books had impressed him, but the original work changed his life.

Shuffling slowly from one canvas to another and back again, and then again, and yet again, barely aware of people or time, Gold stared at the paintings for hours, thrilled and transfixed. He couldn't explain the power of the work to himself except to conclude that here was the exquisite labor of a decent man who saw the world much as he did.

Back home Gold read everything he could find about Van Gogh, and one book by Vincent himself, a collection of his letters to his brother Theo. He was surprised at the excellence of the artist's prose, but wasn't surprised to learn that, though Van Gogh experienced almost no commercial success during his lifetime, prominent painters had respected his work. Whenever Gold read or thought about the nine weeks in 1888 that Vincent had spent with Paul Gauguin in a small yellow house in Arles, France, he was moved to tears of equal parts sorrow and joy. On the streets of Arles boys had thrown rubbish at Van Gogh and verbally abused him.

After years of practicing law, and dealing with inevitable hypocrisies and absurdities, and earning far more money than he would ever need, Gold decided to go somewhere and write his own book, about Vincent Van Gogh. It wouldn't be a mere biography, or a critique of the paintings. He would do his best to explore and define the troubled artist's soul, and to explain why the world had written him off as a peculiar outcast, and, most importantly, what his rejection said about the world. Even before he began work Gold understood that there was little chance he would complete the book to his own satisfaction. He decided before he began not to tell anyone what he was trying to do. Instead, when questioned, he would claim to be writing a book about the law. In the rare chance that he completed his Van Gogh book and judged it satisfactory, he wouldn't submit it for publication. He would set it aside in a safe place, possibly to be appreciated after his death. As had been the case with Vincent, he felt that, ideally, work should be its own reward.

Weightlifting was Gold's only other compelling interest in life. Inflicted with a handicap, he took it up determined to develop the limited physical strength he possessed to its greatest possible potential. He ate the proper foods, and through his high school years spent at least two hours in the gym five days per week. His routine included a half-hour warm up, with the remainder of the time spent with barbells, plates and dumbbells, alternating bicep curls, cross-body curls, bench presses, clean and presses, tricep pushdowns, tricep extensions, lateral raises, pullovers and dead-lifts. As the months and years passed, his muscles, tendons and ligaments inexorably strengthened.

At Columbia Gold lengthened his workouts to three hours per day, four days per week, with three off-days to concentrate on studies and give his muscles the opportunity to grow. Though he never spoke the words aloud and rarely said them to himself, he lived by the age-old and often discredited weightlifting credo: no pain, no gain. He had little difficulty learning to tolerate the agony of muscles gorged with lactic acid and burning like fire, and eventually he learned to enjoy the pain because of the possibilities it represented. Shortly after graduation, before he left on his European trip, he achieved one of his major goals - arm-curling 250 pounds.

Now, living in his yellow trailer in the woods, for five days he worked on his book from daybreak until noon and, after a protein lunch, lifted weights and read books until dinnertime. His days off were spent hiking through the countryside with the aid of an oaken staff. What social life he wanted centered on Mini's tavern, where he met with his friends and trounced Sand at chess.

otro

Leaden rainclouds moved slowly east to west across the sky.

Instead of picking Otro up himself, Sheriff Zouch sent his deputy. Otro watched from his deck when Zach Dipple turned up his driveway shortly before noon. Loot, with a commissioned painting to finish at home, had been gone for over an hour. Before leaving she and Otro had enjoyed a breakfast of venison, mushrooms and coffee, and after that run to a nearby hot springs, soaked themselves, made love, soaked again, and then run back.

As Otro descended his front steps Dipple climbed out of the county SUV. He was a tall man in a light brown uniform with a large nose, pimply white skin, and a small, soft belly sagging over a black leather belt. Under the belly and off to both sides were a weapon and baton in black leather holsters. Staring at Otro, almost seeming to smile, he leaned with his back against his vehicle, arms crossed.

"Come on now," he said. "Climb in back."

"You're late," Otro answered.

"Not my fault. Blame the sheriff. Climb on in. Where's your shoes?"

"I don't wear shoes."

"How come?"

"A lie can travel a thousand miles while the truth wastes time putting its shoes on."

Dipple stared harder at Otro. "Maybe so," he finally said.

Otro slid into the back seat. Black wire mesh separated the back seat from the front. "It stinks in here," he said.

"Three over-dosers puked back there last night. Later on one of 'em died."

"The window won't open."

Dipple backed and turned and headed toward town. "It can't open 'cause it ain't sup*posed* to," he said. "That's 'cause a detainee might jump out an' run away."

"Open your window. Please."

"Nope, can't do it, sorry."

"I need some fresh air. If you don't open your window I'll have to break mine out."

Dipple laughed. "The one back there? No way. That there glass is what they're gonna call Tuffglass. The state's gonna call it that. They gave it to us to try out. Light as a feather an' stronger'n shit is what it is. They guarangoddamnteed it."

Otro knew that products tested by the state in poor rural areas often turned out to be substandard. He slid his t-shirt off, wrapped it tightly around his right hand, and smashed his fist through the tuffglass. The vehicle swerved at the sound and skidded to a stop as Otro unwrapped his fist.

"Son of a *bitch!*" Dipple stood bent at the waist on the roadside looking through the broken window, his face pink. "How'd you *do* that?" he said. "What *happened?*"

"A rock came through the window."

"Bullshit! That glass is rein*forced!*"

"If it's reinforced, how did it break?"

"Lemme see your hand!"

Otro showed his right fist.

"Lemme see that other one!"

"Other what?"

"Hand!"

Otro showed his left fist.

"Son of a *bitch!* Well then where'd the rock *come* from?"

"I couldn't tell where it came from."

"Well where is it? I don't see no rock!"

"I don't see one either. But it might've been a meteorite."

"A what?"

"A fragment of rock or metal from outer space."

"Son of a *bitch*! How come you took your t-shirt off?"

"It was too hot in here with all the windows closed."

Otro pulled his t-shirt on.

Back in the driver's seat, Dipple slammed the door hard. "The sheriff's gonna shit bricks," he said.

"That might be painful."

><

The jail was an old square concrete block building. Directly across the street stood an even older wooden building, with a large black sign over the front door that read ZAP'S PAWN SHOP in white letters. As Dipple turned into the jail lot, two bearded old men wearing overalls and wide-brimmed straw hats walked out of the pawn shop. Behind them, a despondent looking young woman in jeans and a black sweatshirt walked into another ancient wooden building next door with a black sign with white letters over its door reading PETE'S PIZZA PALACE.

Dipple climbed out of the SUV, slammed his door and stared at Otro through the broken window. "Get on out now, get your shoeless self inside."

With Dipple behind him Otro walked between two parked county SUVs and up three concrete steps, where Dipple stepped ahead of him to punch in code numbers on a security lock. Otro followed him through the heavy green steel door that swung open. Inside were six jail cells down each side of a wide corridor, three of them on the left with young brown-skinned men in them. All three stood up from their bunks as Dipple and Otro passed by.

"Three thieves waitin' for justice," Dipple said. "Food's what they stole."

"Estupido culo," one of the prisoners said.

"You talk Spanish?" Dipple asked Otro.

"Yes."

"Well then what'd he say?"

"He was speaking Chinese."

"You tellin' me you speak Chinese?"

"Not that dialect."

On the right-hand side in the last cell down a scrawny old white man in soiled underpants sat on his bunk giving Dipple the finger with both hands.

"Drunk out of his gourd," Dipple said. "Last night he was. Looks like he still is. Third time this week. I feel kinda sorry for 'im. I really do."

The corridor ended at an office with **SHERIFF J. ZOUCH** stenciled on the frosted glass window of the door.

"Go on," Dipple said, "get yourself on in."

Otro opened the door and there was Zouch, eyes squinted, a dour look on his face. His scraggly brown hair reminded Otro of a scrub jay's nest. In front of him on the desktop were a large opened bag of potato chips, a red coffee mug, and a heavy green glass ashtray.

Zouch's sweat-stained wide-brimmed white hat sat next to the ashtray. With a lit cigarette in his hand, Zouch looked past Otro at Dipple. "Saw you arrive," he said. "Any problems?"

"I'm sorry, sir. But a window broke. Back window. Experimental window. I got no idea how the - I got no idea how it happened. It just *did*. I'm sorry. I was watchin' the road, an' *bam*! *Crash*! This here detainee said it was a rock. But there wasn't no rock *in* there. Could a rock break that special glass anyway? He says it could've come from outer space. I mean - "

"Hang up your key," Zouch said.

"Listen, Sheriff Zouch, I - "

"Hang up the key!"

Dipple hung his vehicle key on a pegboard on the wall next to the door. There were other vehicle keys there, along with an oversized antique key that Otro thought might be for the cells.

"Now scram, Dipple."

"But – "

"Vamoose!"

Dipple slipped out and closed the door quietly.

"Sit yourself down, misfit."

"Where?"

"There." Zouch pointed at two gray metal folding chairs leaned against the wall to Otro's right. "Take one and sit."

"No."

"No?"

"I'll stand."

"Well we'll see about that. Yesterday I stopped by that dump where all you weirdos hang out."

When Otro made no answer Zouch twisted his cigarette out in the green glass ashtray and blinked his watery eyes. He shook his head and smiled, opened a side desk drawer and reached in to take out a pack of Pall Malls. Every move was close to slow motion. He tapped the bottom of the pack three times on the desktop, pulled a cigarette out, dropped the pack back into the drawer. Then he lifted out a red and white box of wooden matches. He struck a match with his thumbnail, lit up, inhaled deeply, blew the match out, held it, looked at it, dropped it to the floor, and then blew a cloud of smoke across the desk at Otro.

"Learned how to strike a match that way from my moron wife," he said. "Where were you born, misfit?"

"I don't know."

"How old are you?"

"I'm not sure."

"If you don't know even where you were born, how do you know where you rightly belong?"

"I belong wherever I happen to be."

"You sure as shit don't belong around here. You're a murdering son of a cheap whore is what you are. So tell me why you killed O'brien. Murdered O'brien. He was a successful man, not some worthless misfit weirdo piece of shit like you. I been looking into this thing. Tell me how much his wife Kelly Anne paid you for the job. You tell me that, it'll go a little easier on you. Not a hell of a lot easier but some at least. You got my word."

Otro stared at Zouch.

"You want to do this thing the hard way then?" Zouch said.

Somewhere outside a dog barked. When Zouch blew another cloud of smoke at Otro, Otro blew most of it back.

"Step up here close to the desk, misfit."

Otro stepped forward until his thighs were pressed against the edge of the desk.

"You do piss me off," Zouch said. "You do irritate me, misfit, big time. Compared to you, I'm an important man. Who you are's *no*body! Seems to me you don't understand that, don't quite get it. Put your hand down there flat on the desk."

"Which hand?"

"Right hand'll do."

Otro did it.

"Slide it closer."

Otro did it.

Zouch pressed the burning end of the Pall Mall onto the back of Otro's hand, then twisted it as if he was grinding it out in the ashtray. After he stopped twisting he kept the Pall Mall pressed hard against the hand.

"You like that?" he said.

"Not much," Otro said.

"Well it must hurt some."

Otro made no answer, and his face told Zouch absolutely nothing. Finally the sheriff lifted what was left of the cigarette away, dropped it into the ashtray, smiled at Otro and stood up.

Otro straightened up, staring back at Zouch.

"Turn around," Zouch said. "Face the door."

After he turned, Otro heard Zouch push his chair back and walk around the desk. He heard Zouch slide his baton out of its holster and then heard him grunt.

dipple

Since late in the 19th century Zachariah Webster Dipple's first name had been bestowed upon the first-born male in every Dipple family. The tradition began with the current Zachariah's great-great-great-great-grandfather, Zachariah Luther Dipple, a part-time deputy sheriff who had gleefully overseen the public lynching of eleven "niggers" in and around Gulfport, Mississippi. Back then lynchings were routinely attended by the public, children included, as if they were traveling circuses or carnivals. Every male Dipple who had ever lived was a committed white supremacist, and by the time the current Zachariah reached high school he believed he understood why.

It was, quite simply, looks. Often through the years his father and mother had shown him dozens of photo collections that spanned generations. The photos depicted Dipples at work, play, and celebratory gatherings. In every generation and at all ages the males constituted an exceedingly homely clan. They tended to be puny, with beak-like noses, protruding teeth, and oversized ears and Adam's apples. All the adolescent males displayed harsh cases of acne, from necks to foreheads. They remained puny through young manhood, with small pot bellies and blond hair already beginning to thin. As mature adults the men were bald as hard boiled eggs. Obesity came with early middle-age.

When Zachariah Webster Dipple understood that his family hated other races with unusual ferocity chiefly because they hated themselves, he began to consider running away from home. Racism aside, he thought that escaping the family was bound to lead to a better life somewhere. Anywhere.

The family had been growing feed corn for pigs on their fertile land since the 19th century. Zachariah Webster became the first Dipple to make an effort to find a life of his own. On his eighteenth birthday he packed as many necessities as he could carry into a burlap sack and, wide awake and anxious, sat on his bed with his kid brother Jethro soundly asleep on the bed across the room. Daddy Dipple never retired before midnight, so Zach waited fretfully until two a.m. to make his escape. The only way in or out of the farmhouse was through a trapdoor in the middle of the living room. With the house raised on iron beams, the living room floor was ten meters off the ground, and the only way to the ground, or back up from the ground, was by means of a nine-meter length of thick hemp rope.

The trapdoor had been in use throughout Zach's life. Though Daddy had never been clear about when the house was built, or when it had been elevated, he often ranted, most often at the dinner table, about why the dwelling's unique security features were essential.

"Cain't trust 'em." he always began. "Ever one of 'em would like to wring our white necks. Pump us fulla bullets. They come here from shithole countries where life's worthless. We pay 'em what we got to pay em'. Yes we do. An' most all of 'em don't speak English when we ain't around. I heard 'em lots of times, 'specially out in the fields. They got nothin' to do but wander 'round an' keep a eye on the machines an' they moan an' bitch about that. That's how I see it. That's how it *is!*"

At 2:22 a.m. Zach tiptoed into Daddy's bedroom - Momma slept in her own room across the hall - and he found the wallet he was counting on in the bedside table drawer. He hit it lucky and came away with a wad of $100 bills. Moments before he softly closed the door on his way out, Daddy began to snore. "I hope you croak, you son of a bitch, the sooner the better," his son whispered as he tip-toed down the carpeted hallway.

Zach walked quietly downstairs and took a last look around in the living room. It was overcrowded with old, uncomfortable furniture and, barely visible in the darkness, a super-sized television set in a far corner. There were lethal weapons in drawers and closets for Zach to choose from, and he decided on a compact automatic titanium handgun, lightweight and easily concealed. He slid the weapon and two full ammo clips into his sack.

Then, at the trapdoor, he entered the combination. When the door opened he dropped his sack through and heard it hit the ground in the darkness below. He slid both feet into aluminum stirrups and gripped the hemp rope with one hand and flipped a switch with the other.

Exactly ten meters down his feet touched solid ground, and he slung his sack over his shoulder and walked out from under the farmhouse.

otro

As Otro awakened flat on his back on a sagging cot with his head throbbing, he knew exactly where he was. Before he opened his eyes he recognized odors emanating from damp concrete walls, the cot itself, and a stopped-up toilet. The same dog he'd heard from Zouch's office earlier was barking again.

A dried film of blood on Otro's eyelids cracked when he blinked. Dark watermarks showed on the light gray concrete ceiling. Above him on the wall to his right the sun shone through a small window with three vertical bars. He turned his head to squint at the bright barred square of light on the opposite wall, swung his legs over the edge of the cot, and sat with his feet pressed against the cool concrete floor, elbows on his knees, head in his hands. He carefully picked bits of dried blood from his face, dropped the pieces, and watched them fall and flutter to the floor like tiny black snowflakes.

The man in the neighboring cell asked him, "Estas bien?"

Otro looked at him and smiled. "Si," he said. "No problema."

"Mi nombre es Jesus. Quien eres tu? Who are you?"

"Hola, Jesus," Otro said. "Yo me llamo Otro. I call myself Otro."

"Otro?"

"Si. The Other."

"Via con Dios, Otro."

"Gracias. I'm all right. Estoy bien."

With most of the dried blood removed Otro ran his right hand across the top of his head and touched the swelling just above the hairline behind his right eye. He looked at the back of his right hand. The cigarette burn was raw and red with a narrow circle of lighter red around it.

The dog stopped barking but soon began again when a vehicle passed on the road. Otro thought it possible that Zouch could be surveilling him from his office and sat cross-legged directly under the window with his eyes closed, his back against the wall. He took deep breaths and held them a long time and then exhaled slowly.

A door slammed and Dipple came down the hallway.

"Aqui viene el idiota," Jesus said.

"Hijo de puta," said another voice.

Dipple stopped at Otro's cell and rattled something across the bars. "Hey!" he said. "You wide awake? Hey you!"

"Hola," Otro said.

"Don't try that foreign stuff on me. Get on over here now, the sheriff wants you back. You listen now. I'm sorry he bonked you like he did. I really am, 'cause far as I know he had no call to. That's how I see it anyway. I got my job, you know? But the fact is, I think I might be on your side now."

"I appreciate it."

Otro stood and stepped across the cell and stopped two feet from Dipple, who had trouble fitting the big metal key that he'd rattled against the bars into the lock. When the cell door swung open it made a noise like doors of haunted houses made in old movies.

"Get on back to the sheriff's office now. You gonna be okay? We got a place where there's a nurse. An office on down the road."

"No thanks."

"You got some damn hard bark on you, that's one thing I know."

Prisoners called out as Dipple followed Otro along the hallway:

"Estupido!"

"Hijo de puta!"

"Gilipollas!"

"You maybe better be nicer to Sheriff Zouch," Dipple said. "Friendlier I mean. Can't be easy, but that's my advice. Know what I'm sayin'?"

"Yes, I do."

"I got nothin' against you. Not unless you broke that friggin' window I don't. Hell, even if you did. Break it I mean. Outer space? You're weird, but I got nothin' against you. You believe me?"

"Why should it matter to you what I believe?"

"I got to do my job. Know what I mean? Where'd you learn to talk languages so good? You from some other country someplace? That one thief, your next-door neighbor back there, he calls himself Jesus, claims that's his name. It's true, I saw it on his papers. 'Cept he can't even say it right. Your head looks pretty bad. But you sure ain't the only one who ever had hard times. I had me some too, I kid you not. Get on in there now."

Otro stepped through the office door and closed it behind himself, leaving Dipple in the hallway. Now it felt hot in Zouch's office. The sheriff sat behind his desk. In front of the desk the wooden floor was damp where Otro's blood had been mopped up. On the desktop now was a small stack of papers anchored down by a shiny worn horseshoe. "What happened to your head, misfit? You fall down? You took yourself a fall, right? You better remember that. Busted open your own thick skull. In case somebody asks. Some Jew lawyer maybe."

Zouch again lifted the pack of Pall Malls out of his desk drawer, shook one loose and lit it. This time he reached down to strike the match on the underside of his chair. He inhaled and coughed and blew more smoke at Otro. "Some Jew lawyer might believe your bullshit. Some crippled Jew named Gold. How's your hand, misfit? Show it to me."

Otro held his left hand up.

"The *other* hand. Put it down same way you did before!"

Otro leaned over to press the palm of his right hand next to the papers underneath the horseshoe.

"Does it hurt much?" Zouch asked.

"No."

"Looks to me like you got a pretty nasty burn there. How'd that happen?"

Otro didn't answer.

Zouch sneered, inhaled and coughed, let the smoke out slowly, and then made as if to grind the cigarette onto the back of Otro's hand.

Otro didn't flinch. Zouch stopped the Pall Mall an inch from his skin. "You're gonna die, misfit," he said. "You're gonna die, desperado! Desperado! That's the fuckin' word for misfits like you!"

"You'll die too, along with everyone else on earth. And undoubtedly creatures on any number of other inhabited planets."

"What I mean is, you're gonna die *soon*!"

"When?"

Zouch leaned back and lifted the cigarette to his mouth, inhaled and coughed again, and let the smoke out slowly. "Soon enough," he said. "You can make book on that. Oh yeah you can."

"You'd better give up the cigarettes. You might well have stage four lung cancer by now. Odds are you'll die before I do."

"Bullshit. I hear tell you got yourself a squaw."

Otro didn't answer.

"I've had me some squaw pussy lately. Know why? I got my badge, my power. I'm a man. I might get me some more pretty soon too. Know who I mean?"

"D'imbecil," Otro said.

"What'd you say?"

"Idiot, in French."

Zouch's face reddened. He squashed the cigarette out in the ashtray. "You're gonna die!" he said to Otro. "*Soon!*"

Zouch's phone beeped and he answered at once, staring at the desktop.

"Yeah?... Who?... No fuckin' way!" He hung up. "Now listen to me, desperado. That man you murdered had friends. Big shot friends. I been talking to them. And they're out there looking for *you!* Right now, right this minute. I know it for a fact! Why'd you murder their friend? He was a White Lightning. You know who they are? What they are? Sure you do. Respectable men. Successful men. They ride out here for some innocent fun is all. Also maybe 'cause there's way less traffic than where they come from. So why'd you want to kill O'brien, what'd he ever do to you? Tell me the truth. Somebody pay you off? Somebody like O'brien's wife Kelly Anne? You that hard up for cash? That it? How'd she find you? What's *wrong* with people like you? What I wonder is, how *much* did Kelly Anne pay you to shoot her old man who everybody knew she hated? I could shoot you myself right here an' now an' save the legal system some time and money. But I think I'll turn you loose instead. What I can do then is, I can let O'brien's White Lightning buddies do the job for me. I got a feeling they're all set. Unless you fess up. Want to? That Jew lawyer can't help you once I turn you loose!"

Otro stared blankly at Zouch.

"Talk!" Zouch said.

"Aside from the fact that you're stupid and ugly, and possibly a terminal cancer case by now, what's your major malfunction?"

"I'm a proud American citizen! That's white! A proud *white* American citizen! You know what you are? Fucking *trash! Shit!*"

Zouch grunted when he threw his mug. Otro ducked as it sailed past his head and shattered against the wall behind him. Spilled coffee stained both Zouch's shirt and the papers underneath the horseshoe. He looked at his shirt, then at the papers, then at Otro. *"Dipple!"* he screamed.

Dipple hurried into the office, his eyes on Zouch, whose red face shone with sweat. Zouch rubbed at his coffee-stained shirt with his left hand, his right hand resting on his holstered weapon. "You really think that dirty Jew can help you? Okay, Dipple, take this son of a whore away! Remember what I told you? Yeah you do!" Zouch coughed, then pounded his chest with a clenched fist.

"Okay, boss, but you said - "

"Go! Now! Vamoose!"

jesus

Jesus Herrera was born and raised in the Guatemalan coastal village of Tilipita. By age twelve he was big and strong enough to begin fishing the offshore waters for dorado and tuna from his father's panga. His father, Hector, a resourceful man who at an early age had taught himself to read and write, explained to Jesus all the reasons why fish populations had long been in decline.

As a boy Hector had heard stories from his father about schools of surface-feeding tuna numbering in the thousands. By the time Jesus began to fish there were hundreds of tuna in the largest schools. Hector explained to his son that, even with the oceans dying, fishermen were luckier than most poor people. Ordinary countrymen who lived in cities and worked for either the government or private employers had always been exploited, and always would be. But now, in an economy that needed few workers to support the very few at the top who were rich, millions of ordinary Guatemalans had become irrelevant, and irrelevant was worse than exploited. But despite all that had gone wrong, as long as fish could be taken from the sea people who had to eat would buy them.

Jesus was twenty years old when his father, riding a bicycle loaded down with tuna filets on a dark night along a narrow road toward a neighboring village several kilometers north, was struck and killed by a truck driven by a drunk driver. By the time Jesus took his father's place in the panga - and his younger brother Francisco took his old place - floating islands of discarded trash were commonly seen on the ocean's surface. Schools of tuna were rarely seen and often contained no more than a few dozen fish.

While Jesus and Francisco fished, their mother, Rosa, and their sisters, Maria and Juana, toiled in the family garden, doing their best to raise tomatillos, maiz, chayote, chiles, nopales, and pimientos. But a powerful El Nino had brought on a severe drought, drying up local streams and depleting aquifers. During the unyielding drought there were month-long stretches when clean water became unavailable. The prices of food, clothing and fuel climbed until the brothers, out on the water all day nearly every day, sometimes in dangerous seas, could barely keep the family alive. The prices fishermen received for tuna steadily climbed, but the prices of what they had to buy to sustain families climbed faster. Jesus saw no choice but to try to make his way to America, a country where, word had it, money could still be made by those willing to work at jobs that few Americans would take. He would work there at whatever he could find, wherever he could find it, and send as much money as possible back home.

An old man, a close family friend named Carlos who through a long life had made the trek north and back three times and had finally saved enough money to live his life out in Tilipita, gave Jesus written advice and detailed directions. There were workable strategies, and there were remote routes toward and into America that remained relatively safe. Carlos assured Jesus that, with intelligence and luck, he might well make it, and once safely in America he could find *trabajo sucio* (grubby work) that paid far more than anything he could hope for at home.

Jesus did his best to reassure his family. After he departed, his brother Francisco, as often as he could afford fuel, would continue to fish from the panga. When the sun and moon were aligned to create the lowest tides, he could join the hordes of villagers who searched the beaches for clams.

Jesus set out with moderate confidence and little money. Once across the border into Mexico, he passed through drought-stricken country for two months. After that there were about three thousand kilometers more to the border. Three thousand kilometers was less than two thousand miles, so he decided to think of the distance in miles to make it seem shorter. Other desperate men and women were making the same trek, but Carlos had advised him that traveling with strangers could be dangerous and that a lone man attracted less attention.

Due to daytime temperatures that reached 115 degrees, Jesus travelled mostly at night, taking occasional rides when he was lucky enough to get them. He walked at least half the distance, climbed mountains and waded streams, slept alone in wild country, begged for food or stole it when he could. He believed stealing food was more honorable than begging and that there was more honor in stealing from large farms than from family fields. Whenever he had extra food he packed it in a plastic sack and, when he could get it, carried drinking water in a plastic bottle.

During his journey he came upon desiccated corpses, skin dry as parchment stretched over yellowed bones, clothing rotted to tatters and threads. In the state of Zacatecas Jesus appropriated a pocketknife from underneath a skeletal corpse sprawled facedown a few yards from a dry creek bed.

He followed Carlos' precise written directions. By the time he neared the American border he had lost count not only of days and weeks, but of months. Shortly before dawn, not long after a rainstorm, exactly where Carlos had indicated it would be, he finally saw a border wall from two kilometers away. In this remote desert nothing manmade besides the wall was visible in any direction.

Jesus sat waiting, back against a rock ledge, shaded by brittlebush. In the afternoon heat a small airplane flew slowly back and forth along the wall at low elevation and then, after an hour, disappeared. An hour later from somewhere across the wall a distant siren sounded briefly. By late in the evening Jesus had been joined by three men and two women, one of the women with a five-year old son, and, the last to arrive, a wiry, white-haired old man. Everyone was nervous, friendly, hungry and tired. They shared their food and water and talked, mostly about where they had come from and the loved ones they'd left behind.

Shortly before dark a discussion began, and then an argument, about what the most successful way to attempt a border crossing would be. Two men shouted confusing and contradictory advice. When they stopped shouting, Jesus told the group what he'd learned from Carlos. Here in this lonely place surveillance was minimal. Though the American government issued propaganda about guarding their borders, they spent little money on security. In America, as the whole world knew, everything had always been about money, saving it, making it or stealing it. There were still American bosses who needed workers willing and able to accept low pay and who, out of fear, never complained to anybody and stayed out of trouble with the law. It had always been that way. Workers who didn't avoid trouble helped fill the prisons, which themselves were money-making enterprises.

Finally, when darkness fell, Jesus offered to lead the group to the tunnel that Carlos and thousands of others had been using for decades. Once they were safely into America, they could rest until morning and then set out in small groups, or alone, in their chosen directions.

With more or less enthusiasm, everyone agreed.

Jesus led them to the tunnel, which began as a narrow hole in sandy soil between two massive boulders, exactly as Carlos had described it. The group entered in single file, Jesus leading the way. It was a dark, slow hour-long-bent-at-the-waist walk, downwards, then level, then back up, and, except for occasional prayers and curses, they made their way in silence.

Finally they emerged into desert air that smelled clean after the cave. Jesus told them again that the smart thing to do was rest until first light, and then survey the countryside and choose their routes northward. Whenever possible they should stay close to cover so they could quickly hide themselves at any sign of danger.

Traveling alone, Jesus rode, walked, worked and stole his way northward, then turned west. Every day he thought about Tilipita and his people there, and at night he had them in his dreams. He also dreamed about hooking tuna, hauling them over the gunwale and into the panga, their sides flashing silver under the sun.

otro

As Dipple made a slow right turn out of the parking lot, three men dressed like old-time movie cowboys crossed the street toward the pawn shop, making Otro wonder whether it might be Halloween.

"See that one in the fancy pink shirt?" Dipple said. "What's he going in a pawn shop for? What he does is, he sells dope. Big time. Uppers, downers, in-betweeners, everything, the works. His rich old man sells dope wholesale. The kid sells it like a hobby, on the street. Likes to drug the girls up so he can have his way. I know a sister. Victim's sister I mean. Rape victim I mean. The old man hired big time lawyers to get his kid, that pink-shirt one, off. They never even staged a trial. I'd sure like to know what that dude needs in a pawn shop. Maybe a gun. You sure enough got a Jew lawyer? You figure he can get you off? You can talk to me. You figure I'm your enemy? Not me. No way. I got a job an' all I do is what I get told to do. That's all."

"You'd have done well in Germany in the 1930s."

"Way back then? What's that mean? You know what? A loony down south, maybe South Carolina. Or Georgia. Alabama? Wherever it was, he shot up a house filled with your people, brown-skins I mean. There's loony people out there, all over. How come you can't be friendly to me? I'm not mean. What was it happened in Germany way back when?"

"People did what they were told to do."

"Well what's so wrong with that?"

Otro didn't answer. Warm air streamed through the smashed window. His head throbbed under his wound. Dipple turned east. When they passed the tavern Mini's car was the only one in the lot.

Two miles beyond the tavern three White Lightnings appeared behind them. The rush of air through the smashed window covered the sound of their machines, so by the time Otro heard them they were riding in a tight group, side by side, fifteen or twenty yards back, their bikes billowing clouds of black exhaust. Otro remembered what Alejandro had once told him, that many White Lightnings customized their exhaust systems in order to leave clouds of filth behind them wherever they went.

"Looks like we got us company," Dipple said. "Not my fault. You want to blame somebody, blame ol' Zouch."

Otro took a long look at the White Lightnings. All three were big men well on their way to fat, wearing shiny black helmets. There was no way Otro could tell whether or not they were armed. He wondered how ineffectual they were and knew he'd find out soon.

"No way this here is my fault," Dipple said. "You got to believe that."

They passed an old cemetery on the right-hand side of the road. The graves were tightly spaced rows of shallow indentations in weedy earth. All the tombstones were small and many appeared to be missing. Beyond the graves they crossed a narrow wooden bridge over a creek and after that entered a forest. Contained by trees, the motorcycles sounded louder. Out ahead of them a gray squirrel started across the road, stopped near the middle, turned as if to head back, and then stopped and froze. Dipple swerved to miss the little animal.

"I got nothin' against them squirrels," he said.

Little sunlight penetrated the trees. They crossed another bridge over another creek and a mile later an old cattle guard crossed the road. Not far beyond the cattle guard was government land where loggers had clear-cut the hillsides long ago.

Dipple would have to slow down to pass over the cattle guard. The hole in the window Otro had shattered was barely big enough for him to fit his head through. He began removing shards and slivers of residual glass and placed the pieces beside him on the seat. Before they reached the cattle guard he worked the last sizeable fragment out of the window frame. He could see bright light down the road where the forest ended.

Small glass cuts had drawn blood on his left hand and he smeared it across the back of Dipple's seat. Out ahead two ravens sailed side by side from a tree limb to glide across the road, and a third bird followed close behind them. As Dipple began to slow down Otro gripped the bottom window frame with both hands. Then came rapid jolts from the cattle guard rails. He put his head and shoulders through the window, planted his feet on the seat, and pushed with all his leg-strength. His left thigh banged against the window frame and then he was into the air.

He heard the motorcycles roar and smelled their foul exhaust. He hit the ground on his side, rolled onto his knees and pushed to his feet and ran hard. By the time the White Lightnings had cut their engines he was nearly to the trees.

"Halt!" Dipple yelled behind him. "Hey, man, halt!"

"Son of a bitch!" a White Lightning yelled.

Otro sprinted over the fir and pine needle floor of the forest. Before a half minute had passed he knew he was far enough into the trees to watch and wait. He stood among sword ferns close to a ponderosa pine.

The White Lightnings were after him. Their engines frequently revved as they rode their machines through the forest in single file. They made slow uphill progress through the trees. Far behind them Otro saw Dipple start back toward town at a moderate speed.

When the White Lightnings were close enough Otro stepped out of the ferns and waved his arms at them. Concentrating on the unfriendly terrain, they didn't see him. He cupped his hands around his mouth and screamed, but they didn't hear him over the noise of their machines. There were no rocks to be found so Otro pried a chunk of thick bark from the side of the pine, took aim and heaved it at the lead rider. When the chunk turned end-over-end and struck him on the upper thigh he came to a sudden stop. When the White Lightning saw him Otro waved as if in friendly greeting.

He was ready to disappear behind the pine if a weapon appeared, but all the White Lightning did was scream:

"*Motherfucker!*"

Otro started uphill at a walking pace through the cinnamon-colored trunks of the ponderosas. As the White Lightnings followed through tall trees and deadfall and protruding roots and patches of sword fern he checked back over his shoulder and slowed down three times so as not to lengthen his lead.

The hill gradually steepened. It was cool and dark in the shade of trees. Otro didn't want them to quit the chase, so he slowed again to allow them to close the distance. When the leader was twenty yards behind, Otro saw his sweaty face and heard him scream: "We're gonna end you, halfbreed! *End* you, motherfucker!"

Otro climbed the hill, maintaining his lead.

On a steep slope the Harley motors howled, their rear wheels spinning uselessly in the decomposing duff of the forest floor. They could go no further. When they cut their engines the silence seemed complete. Two of them sat side by side a few yards behind the leader, all three looking at Otro as he stood looking down at them.

The leader screamed again: "We're gonna fuckin' *end* you!"

"No you're not," Otro answered.

The leader slid from his seat and stood there in his baggy black pants with his arms crossed, sneering at Otro. The two behind him, one wearing a heavy silver chain around his neck, climbed off their Harleys.

"Get that fucking halfbreed!" the leader screamed.

All three lifted their helmets off and hung them by the chinstraps on their handlebars.

Otro smiled at them and turned his back and began climbing the hill. He chose the roughest available terrain, and moved slowly enough to let them think they might catch up.

"Fucking halfbreed!"

"Cocksucker!"

"Motherfucker!"

Ten minutes into the climb Otro could hear them wheezing and panting. He slowed until the leader closed the distance between them to five yards. When he snarled at him Otro laughed and turned to climb, angling between trees and circling patches of brush. A quarter mile from the summit the trees thinned and large patches of warm sunlight reached the forest floor.

Otro came to a deadfall fir, its trunk four feet thick. He stopped again, turned to face the White Lightnings and hopped onto the trunk and jogged uphill over the rough bark toward the exposed tangle of roots. When he looked back he saw three exhausted men bent at the waist, elbows braced against their knees. He hopped off the trunk on the far side of the tree and ran back downhill.

They screamed and cursed as he passed them by.

Not far below the White Lightnings a ruffed grouse flushed with a roar from a thick clump of brush and set its stubby wings to glide downhill through the trees. Otro ran through fern and over spongy moss and soon saw the grouse he'd flushed perched on the low limb of a cedar. This was country he loved and Otro felt happy in it. He slowed to a walk to take his bearings. The exertion had his head bleeding again, and he took a patch of cool, damp moss from a cedar trunk and pressed it tightly against the wound. When he reached the three Harleys he ripped out their hoses and wires.

><

With the moss pressed against his wound Otro walked along the right-hand shoulder of the road. He considered running to Sand's dwelling but decided to save time and energy by hitching a ride and giving the bleeding time to stop.

He'd been walking no more than half an hour when he heard a vehicle behind him and stopped on the roadside to wait. A pharmaceutical delivery truck began to slow long before it reached him. When it stopped beside him the rider gazed out the open window, sizing him up.

"You hurt bad?" he said.

"No," Otro said, "but I'd be thankful for a ride."

"How far?"

"To a few miles this side of the village."

"Village? I guess you got a point. It ain't much of a town, is it? Except for the pharma warehouse it ain't. I'm picking up a load of meds. Hop on in."

Otro hopped in. The driver was middle-aged with thin blond hair combed sideways over a bald spot. He wore overalls and on top of them a pink t-shirt with two lines of small letters in bright red print across the chest:

*time goes about its immemorial task of
making everyone look and feel like shit.*

The driver's right cheek bulged with chewing tobacco. As the truck pulled away and picked up speed he spat a stream of brown juice out his window.

"Name's Fergy," he said.

"Otro."

"Otro?"

"Otro."

"Your name?"

"My name."

"I know you," he said. "Seen you before."

"Where?"

"That joint down the road out by that lake. Or pond. Whatever it is. Where that oddball lady tends bar. What's her name?"

"Mini."

"Yeah, yeah, Mini. Mini's all right. Kinda strange but nice. I stop in now an' again for a beer when it's open, when the time's right. She lets us drivers in sometimes. I mean, beer's about free there. That's where I seen you, must've been three, four years ago. You were in there with some others like yourself. I remember faces good but I ain't worth jack shit with names. Tell me somethin'."

"What?"

"Just curious is all. Where you from?"

"Lots of places."

Fergy glanced sideways. "That don't exactly make sense. What I mean is, where you *from*? What place? Everybody's from someplace, right?"

"Not necessarily."

Fergy looked again. "Now that *truly* don't make sense. Everbody's born someplace. So I'm askin' you where were you born."

"I was too young to know where I was when I was born."

"Okay. Okay. I give up."

They rode in silence for a while.

"How'd you hurt your head?"

"A sheriff hit me with a baton. I stopped the bleeding but then it started again."

"You mean Zouch? Sheriff Zouch did that?"

"Do you know him?"

"Yeah I do. Know *of* 'im. Know enough to hate the evil son of a bitch. I sure as shit remember *his* name. I hate *all* small town cops anywhere. Most anywhere anyhow. Most city cops too for that matter. But small town cops are worst. Anyway, I been on this road right here for lotsa years. Zouch don't dare to screw with pharma trucks. Way back in the day cops set speed traps for log-truck drivers through here though. They fucked my granddaddy over plenty. So fuck all cops includin' Zouch's what I say. How come Zouch whomped you on the bean?"

"He doesn't like me."

"I already figured that much out. How come though? What'd you do?"

"I insulted him."

"Why'd you do that?"

"Why not?"

Half a mile ahead three turkey vultures turned in tight circles close over the road.

"Well now," Fergy said. "I got to back up some. He *is* the law. I mean, Zouch's the fuckin' law. You got to admit that much. I hate his evil guts but he's still the law. Around here he is. We got to respect the law. For our own good we do. We even got to respect Zouch even if we hate his guts. Respect 'im to his *face* I mean. Only to his ugly face. Right?"

"I don't respect him," Otro said. "I pity him."

Fergy spat another stream. "Well I don't pity him," he said.

The turkey vultures had dropped to feed on a road-killed jack rabbit. As the truck neared them the birds aired their wings and waddled slowly, reluctantly away. The last bird in the line of three looked back at the truck.

"Ain't they ugly?" Fergy said. He spat again. "Ain't they though?"

"All they are is what they're meant to be."

"What's *that* mean?"

"I don't see them as any uglier than we are."

"Speak for yourself on that one. Who the hell *are* you? Tell me how come you say weird shit an' disagree all the time."

"I don't."

"Hell if you don't. You jus' did."

"I'll gladly exit your truck if you want."

"I don't mind you bein' in my truck. Jus' tryin' to figure you out is all. It's a hobby I got. Figurin' people. I'm lonely so I got to have a hobby, to pass the time."

"I happen to have the same hobby. I just finished figuring three people out before you picked me up. Three motorcycle riders. Now I'm doing my best to figure you out. There's something synthetic about you."

"I ain't even gonna ask what *that* means. If it does. Mean anything I mean. You got a job?"

"Yes."

"Well what is it?"

"I'm self-employed. I guide people."

"What's that mean?"

"People pay me to take them hunting and fishing."

"No shit? Sounds pretty damn sweet to me. I got a good enough job too, sittin' with pharma all up and down the mountains, over to the coast. People do need their meds, their drugs. Like my shirt says, they mostly look and feel like shit. Lucky for me they built a damn warehouse here. My granddaddy wasn't so lucky. The old-time envirofreaks got it to where they couldn't hardly cut trees down. Still can't far as that's concerned. Hardly any sawmills left. Hardly any *trees* left. So anyhow, the tree-huggers got my granddaddy tossed out on his ass. You a tree-hugger by any chance?"

"Not literally. But I empathize."

"There you go again. You *what?* What the fuck's *that* mean?"

"It means I'm thankful for trees," Otro said.

When Fergy spat again and a few drops of tobacco juice dribbled over his lower lip and down his chin he wiped it off with the back of his hand and wiped the hand on his overalls. "You tellin' me you're what some folks call a liberal?"

"Do you know what the word 'liberal' means?"

"Yeah I do. If you are one it means you're a socialist."

"Do you know what 'socialist' means?"

"A communist. Or right next door to bein' one. People been knowin' that a long time. My daddy knew that much. *His* daddy knew that much."

"Can you define communism?"

"Why the hell should I?"

The truck slowed. "I'd kick your sorry ass if I could," Fergy said.

"You're a fool," Otro said.

The truck stopped.

"Outta my truck! This truck's *mine! Out!*"

Otro nodded at him and smiled. "Thanks kindly," he said. He opened the door, dropped down to the road, waved at Fergy with one hand and shut the door gently with the other.

fergy

In a 1950 children's story author Dr. Seuss occupied a fictional zoo with creatures he called "nerds." Later in the century that name came to be commonly applied to intellectual, socially awkward humans. The fundamental principle in Sean Ferguson's life (no one called him

Fergy then) was his loathing of nerds. He believed that due to their neurotic brain power nerds had relentlessly contaminated the earth and annihilated its myriad inhabitants. Their inventions and ideas produced the industrialization that compelled people to live unnaturally in overcrowded cities. The industries for which workers were forced to labor at monotonous physical tasks polluted the land, air and water, eventually perverting climate itself. Then the artificial technology created and applied by nerds idled workers, thereby producing neurosis, obesity and deadly addictions. And advanced weapons conceived and controlled by nerds maimed and murdered innocent victims everywhere.

Both Fergy's parents had died while he was a teenager. His father, a nerd dedicated to marketing junk food, weighed 352 pounds at age 43 and, while climbing a short flight of stairs at work – the elevator had inexplicably malfunctioned that morning – collapsed in his tracks due to cardiac arrest. By the time his massive body rolled and bounced back down the stairs and several yards across the lobby floor he was dead. Three months later, Fergy's mother slit her own throat in a bathtub, where, soon after arriving home from school, Fergy discovered her body submerged in a foamy pink froth. The neatly printed note on the toilet seat lid read:

The time is out of joint so I've decided to leave the joint. (I think I read that in a book somewhere, probably a novel, but nobody can arrest me for plagiarism now.) Be careful, son, and please begin thinking things through. Start by reading books I've recommended to you.

Fergy lived with a widowed aunt until his high school graduation. Whether at school or in his cramped room, he spent nearly all his free time reading authors from the distant past whose books his mother had saved and treasured. His favorite authors included Aristotle, Homer, Marcus Aurelius, Shakespeare, Cervantes, Tolstoy, Dostoyevsky, Goethe, Nietsche, Thoreau, Twain, and Orwell.

After high school graduation Fergy began by doing odd jobs requiring rudimentary forms of day labor. He thought hard about somehow fashioning a tolerable life and toward this end devised a persona: he presented himself as a dimwit to anyone he met or came to know. If people regarded him as an irritating if laughable fool, nobody anywhere could ever blame him for anything related to a world destroyed by nerds.

newt

Otro's luck held.

As Fergy's truck pulled away, a rusty paint-peeled van at least a half century old sped down the road. Otro couldn't see the driver through the windshield reflecting sunlight, but, as the van slowed, he held out his thumb and smiled at the glare.

The driver turned out to be a clean-shaved young man with curly blond hair wearing a bright yellow shirt with its long tail hanging out over faded jeans. He motioned Otro to get in. "What's up?" the driver asked.

"How'd you come to get out of a truck way out here? I know that truck. Fergy dropped you off, right?"

"He wanted me out of the truck."

"He the one who smacked you upside the head?"

"Oh no."

"That head looks pretty bad."

"I'll be fine."

"How come he wanted you out?"

"I asked him some questions he couldn't answer."

By now Fergy was a mile or more down the road ahead of them.

"I'm curious. Can't help it. What kind of questions you talkin' about?"

"The definitions of words."

As they picked up speed the driver looked at Otro with a sociable smile. "Don't ask me any questions," he said. "No definitions. Okay?"

"Agreed."

"Pretty quick, we'll pass that moron. Hope you don't mind. One thing I hate's slow vehicles. My name's Newt. I guarantee you you'll get wherever you're goin' faster with me than you would've with Fergy. I keep this jalopy souped up. It's a serious hobby. Ready for some serious speed?"

"Your neck's in here too."

They quickly gained ground on Fergy.

"Where you headed?" Newt asked.

"Up the road a ways."

"Wherever it is, we'll be there soon enough."

When Newt pulled out to make his pass the left-side tires skidded on the dirt and gravel shoulder. "No sweat," he said as he swerved back onto the right-hand lane and accelerated. "I'm a truck driver myself. Today's my day off."

"Keep something in mind," Otro said. "When a German named Benz invented cars in 1886 he made it possible for us to crash and die."

"Not me!" Newt said. "No way. I'm a bonafide expert. I *love* drivin' on my days off. Drivin' my souped up van here. Sure beats sittin' on my butt doin' nothin' in a truck. What else could I do on my day off anyway? Lotsa money goes into this here means of transportation. Truth is I might be, probably am, the best truck driver in these parts. Maybe the best damn truck driver anywhere. I dearly love hittin' the road at two a.m. on a summer mornin' to pick up a load of who the hell knows what. Know why I like it so much?"

"Why?" said Otro.

"Stuff I deliver ends up making people feel fine. Great even, sometimes. I mean, without us truckers, citizens wouldn't get what they want. What they *need*!"

They were speeding between two recently burned over hillsides.

"Only problem is," Newt said, "I got a twin brother. Want to know why it's a problem?"

"If you want to tell me."

Now they were back among scrawny second-growth firs.

"Why you think I'd ask if I didn't want to? Why you figure riders like me pick people like you up? When we're all alone in a truck, or alone like in the van here, we like to talk is why. I sure do. Who doesn't?"

Now on a straight flat stretch of road they were traveling at least one hundred miles per hour.

"Pardon my French," Newt said, "but my twin brother's a goddamn asshole. Identical twin he is. His name's Nathan. Nate. *That's* the problem. *My* problem. What it is, he defies the laws of genetics. He's an evil son of a bitch and a truck driver too. An' the point is, he's mean to people. I mean *mean!* He's even mean to strangers. *Especially* strangers. Like, he'll tell a waitress who serves him his coffee she's a dog. Or a skank. Or he'll ask her why she wastes her time smearing lipstick on a sow. So guess what happens. I go someplace for coffee where Nate's been before me, maybe a day before me, a *week* before even, an' I'll give a waitress my best smile and ask her how she is and how's her day goin', an' she'll make a mean face at me. Sometimes she'll even refuse to serve me. So that means Nate got there before me and treated that waitress like shit. We look *exactly* alike, my evil asshole brother an' me. *Nobody* can tell us apart. One time I pulled in for coffee up there at Dry Creek. You know Dry Creek?"

"Yes."

"One time when I pulled in there Hormel – you know Hormel?"

"I know who he is."

"Hormel wouldn't even serve me. Told me he refused to do business with anybody who called him a motherfucker. That's one word I never use, never say, ever – motherfucker. Turned out Nate called him a motherfucker two days before I got there. I know he didn't have any *reason* to call ol' Hormel a motherfucker. I *know* he didn't have a reason to. Hormel's okay. Anyway, I *never* say motherfucker."

"Do you know the old logging road that branches east over the top of the hill up ahead?"

"I know every road there is in these parts."

"I'd like to get off there."

"At that ol' loggin' road?"

"Yes."

"Why you want off there?"

"Why not?"

"Nobody uses that road anymore's why not. Nobody's used that ol' road for nobody knows how long."

"That's where I want off, and I appreciate the ride."

"What'd you say your name was again?"

"I didn't say. Here comes my road."

"Yeah, I know, I see it. I been told my great-granddaddy hauled logs on that road. Hauled enough logs on that ol' road to build a small town. A *medium* size town. So I been told."

The van came to a stop a few feet beyond the intersection with the logging road. Otro opened the door, hopped out and slammed the door shut, and Newt pulled away.

These days the logging road was used by occasional deer and elk poachers in fall and winter. It passed through clear-cuts, burnt stretches and stands of stunted fir, and finally dead-ended near the summit of a steep hill. From the summit a narrow switchback trail descended toward what Otro called the village.

nate

Newt's twin brother Nate, kindhearted and popular as a teenager, wanted to help his twin, who had always been extremely introverted. Called on in class, Newt often blushed and fell speechless. He could never work up enough nerve to approach girls, had no close friends, and very few casual acquaintances. Nate came up with a desperate idea – he would create a downward comparison by temporarily turning himself into a malicious jerk, thereby helping his fragile twin gain confidence. The unique strategy was simple. He would irritate people, even enrage them, by telling them the honest truth. His first trial run was with his girlfriend, whom he'd lately grown bored with anyway. On a Friday morning in a school hallway she told him she was wondering whether her new hairdo made her face look heavier. "It makes your face look downright fat," Nate told her. "Makes you look like Petunia Pig. You heard of Petunia? A long time ago she was the girlfriend of a pig named Porky in comic books. Mind if I call you Petunia? Like as a pet name?" They broke up then and there. That evening Nate's mother asked him which he liked best, her tacos or enchiladas, and he told her that in all honesty he didn't much like anything she cooked. A day later he received a handwritten note from his Aunt Carlotta inviting him to spend a weekend with her and Uncle Chase at their mountain cabin near Sugar Pine Lake, and Nate immediately wrote back: "I like lakes and mountains well enough, but nowhere near enough to spend a weekend with you."

Nate gratuitously affronted strangers with insults that stunned and silenced most of them. When an elderly gentleman on a busy street asked him directions, he answered that he had no idea where the Golden Dragon Chinese restaurant was, but if he got directions from someone else and found the place, he should celebrate by taking a flying fuck at a rolling donut. A pleasant lady in a small crowd waiting to get into a popular restaurant asked him why he looked so sad, and Nate's immediate reply was that his first glance at her had done the job. Glaring at him, she stomped her foot against the sidewalk with such force that the high heel of her stylish right shoe broke off.

Nate's transformation did nothing to help Newt, who, on his own, eventually overcame his commonplace adolescent insecurities. But from the very start, probably because for the first time in his life people were paying attention to him, Nate enjoyed being a loathsome jerk, a heartless son of a bitch, and decided to remain one forever.

Word of his peculiar conduct spread quickly. After high school graduation his father wanted Nate out of the house and used his connections to find him a long haul truck driving job. He soon earned reputations as both a first-rate driver and an asshole. During his ninth year on the job a mid-level executive heard about Nate's temperament and called him into his office for an interview. The executive, an ignorant political hack of high standing in his party, wasn't disappointed. Nate - crude, sarcastic, aggressive, quick-witted too – was indeed a world class jerk and clearly reveled in it. He knew how to insult people, laugh at them, call them names, demean them. After some painstaking grooming, and inventing a suitable past for him, party functionaries decided Nate was ready. Most political polls revealed that majorities of voters in rural districts were mad at crime, at immorality, at minorities, at high prices, at endless rules and regulations, at taxes that supported deadbeats and losers, at a world that didn't give decent white Americans what they deserved. Disillusioned voters would regard Nate as a man capable of expressing their impotent rage. The party began planning a well-financed run against Joe Zouch, who, though stupid, was too full of himself to take advice from anybody. If Nate beat Zouch in the primary he'd run against a hopeless liberal fool in the general election, and that would send the loudmouthed asshole all the way to Washington, D.C.

otro

Five years earlier Sand had purchased three acres of land near Frog Creek from a widow, and then a dilapidated manufactured home on wheels from a young man who needed money to make a down payment on his wife's medical bills. Out of kindness, Sand insisted on paying twice the asking price of the mobile home, and used Alejandro's truck to haul it to his property. Because it was rumored to be an Indian burial site the acreage had been cheap.

With Alejandro's help Sand placed what became his home on a solid foundation and painted it bright green. He grew vegetables in a large garden and marijuana in a smaller adjacent plot. His water source was a perennial spring and he heated with an Osburn woodstove. The year after he settled in, Sand flew to Madrid solely to spend a week in the Reina Sofia Museum, where more than one hundred Picassos are on permanent display. He came home with enough high-quality Picasso prints to cover his walls.

As Otro crossed the grassy field he heard the rasp of steel against stone and then in the distance saw Sand sitting on a stump, sharpening a large knife. When he saw Otro coming he stood and waved, then frowned as Otro slowed to a jog. "What happened to your head?"

"Zouch."

"Come on in."

Inside Otro stopped to look at a new Picasso print.

"The Blue Room," Sand said.

"I recognized it. Do you have a favorite?"

"Two," he said. "Guernica and Child with a Dove. They make a powerful combination. Contrast I should say. Sit, please. Let's check that messed up cranium."

Otro sat on an upholstered wooden chair underneath The Blue Room. Sand leaned close, squinting through his wire rimmed glasses. "No problema. I'll shave some hair and suture it up."

He poured water from a glass jug into a stainless steel pot, put the pot on his propane stove and turned the burner to high.

"Gold tells me you might be in some serious trouble."

"Possibly," Otro said.

"I believe it. I'd guess Zouch is clinically insane to some degree and therefore dangerous. You know that of course."

"One thing I need to do now is stay out of sight for a while. When the time comes if it does Gold says he'll help me with the law."

"And Zouch is the local law. We'll all help you any way we can. You can stay here if you want, for as long as you want."

"That could make trouble for you. I can live alone as long as I need to in open country. When I leave here I'll pick Eagle up at Loot's and head out."

While Sand scrubbed his hands at the kitchen sink Otro told him about his ride with Spurmeister, and Hatch's burial.

"Where'd they bury him?"

"Not far from here. About two miles east of Pilgrim Rock."

"Alejandro told me Zouch is paid off by local heroin carriers. Meth dealers? One or the other. He heard it from his friends."

"How do his friends know?"

"According to Alejandro, moronic gringos don't think Spanish speakers can comprehend English. Local carriers pay off Zouch – as if he needs the money - but they fight amongst themselves. This water's warm. I'll shave some hair, clean you up and trim some skin. It won't hurt much. There's a good blood supply to the head and that hastens healing. The stitches can come out in five or six days. I'm using monofilament fishing line, two-pound test. You'll need me or somebody else to remove them."

"Could I do it myself with a mirror?"

"You could, with care and a small, sharp scissors."

Sand draped a clean white towel around Otro's shoulders, then washed his head with a soft cloth soaked in warm, soapy water, and finally used a straight razor to shave off hair.

"What did he hit you with?"

"His baton, from behind. I suppose he swung sidearm."

After the shave Sand carefully cleaned the wound again. While he worked, Otro studied a Picasso print of a boy leading a horse. Sand gently blotted his head with the towel. "I'll trim the skin. Did you hear about the latest mud slide?"

"No."

"Down south, over on the coast."

Sand took the scissors from a kitchen drawer and then showed Otro a larger instrument from the same drawer. "A hemostat," he said. "To secure the needle while I make the stitches."

Otro counted eleven stitches.

"Hurt much?"

"Enough."

"They'll hurt more coming out. Now an antibiotic ointment."

Sand applied the ointment, then a layer of soft gauze, and finally adhesive tape.

"Dizzy? Nausea?"

"No."

"Hungry?"

"Yes."

"Beer?"

"Yes, thanks."

"Go on outside. I'll be with you in a minute."

Outside Otro sat cross-legged near the chopping block. It was pleasant under the sun and comfortably cool whenever a massive cumulus cloud drifted by overhead. High in the sky was a thin expanse of wildfire smoke. A lone hawk circled between the smoke and the clouds. Sand came out with smoked trout, dried peaches and pears, and bottles of beer on a crude wooden tray. He sat on the chopping block and set the tray on the ground between them. As more clouds arrived Otro felt the temperature drop and smelled the rain coming and then noticed that the hawk had disappeared. "Delicious trout," he said. "Cutthroats?"

"Yes. Tell me though. I can't help being curious. Do you truly enjoy being a hunting and fishing guide?"

"I only accept clients I want to be with. Or to be honest I should say clients I don't mind being with. No meat hogs and not very many drunks. No mean drunks. The fishing is mostly catch and release. I charge my clients plenty and they get more than their money's worth. It's what I have and I'm good at it."

"Listen to me, Otro. Come out here whenever you want. Zouch has never been here. I doubt if he knows or cares where I live. If he ever finds out and decides to visit we'll hear him coming from a long way off. One question. Tell me the truth. Would you kill him if you had to?"

"If I had to, yes."

"Have you killed people?"

"Only the two people who tried to kill me. I'll get on my way now. I'm heading for the town. A quick visit. It's time to create diversions. To make things happen. To mix things up. To confuse the issue. Thank you very much for everything."

sand

Heredity is a potent force and genes can travel anywhere. Sand had no way of knowing that he and Deputy Zach Dipple were half-brothers. In Gulfport, Mississippi, sixteen years before Dipple was born, his future daddy impregnated a young Catholic prostitute who had carelessly miscalculated her safe time of month.

She bore her infant son and gave him up for adoption, and before a year had passed he became Jacob Sand, an only child raised by prosperous parents in Boise, Idaho. In due course Sand graduated from Stanford Medical School and went on to establish his lucrative career as a cardiothoracic surgeon.

Beginning with early adolescence Jacob desperately searched for girlfriends but never found one. When he turned fourteen an orthodontist replaced his protruding teeth with implants, but it didn't help. The girls he was attracted to nearly always fell for athletes, even the dumbest athletes, and he tried but failed at everything athletic. He was too small for football and lacked the hand-eye coordination for either basketball or baseball. He tried running, both cross-country and track, but had neither speed nor endurance. A few somewhat homely girls accepted first dates with him, and, after smoking high-powered weed, two of them were willing to make out, but neither agreed to a second date.

By the time he graduated high school at the top of his class Sand was spending most of his free time reading books, watching movies and television, and scrolling his phone. The result was that he never knew what to talk about when he found himself face to face with a live human being. He had few acquaintances and no authentic friends, and three enrollments for six-week programs at an expensive Tech Addict Recovery Treatment Center failed to help.

Whenever Sand was anywhere near attractive women he found himself imagining their naked bodies.

In universities a majority of those who desire sex get something approaching what they want, but a neurotic Sand never got much of anything. As an undergraduate he established a practice of studying seriously all week long, getting drunk or stoned on Friday afternoons, then walking around likely neighborhoods after dark searching for parties. When he found the right kind of party he furtively joined the crowd and looked for drunk or stoned women. Occasionally he encountered a likely target, but none of his adventures ended well.

When he became a successful surgeon, Sand's sex life began at last. At work he was required to talk at length to both doctors and nurses, and many of the nurses, once he worked up the courage to ask them out, ended up letting Sand have his way. He began to believe he might find an acceptable degree of happiness. As his self-confidence grew he prowled the hospital hallways and lounges, head thrust forward like a bird dog seeking the scent of upland game. The game he sought was nurses, and he found them.

Once his sex life was established, it was nearly as structured as his surgery schedule. He engaged in dozens of brief affairs that ranged from a week or ten days to no more than a month. Then, during his third summer of virility, a new nurse appeared at the hospital, a lovely, statuesque creature, half white and half Latina. The first time Sand saw Josephina sipping a cup of espresso in the penthouse lounge he became equal parts captivated and intimidated. Her extreme beauty brought back his feelings of inadequacy, or unworthiness, and it was more than two months after he first saw her that he asked her out to dinner at Reminiscence, a fashionable retro restaurant-nightclub. She was alone and sipping espresso in the penthouse lounge again, and she accepted his invitation with a nod of her head and a friendly smile.

By the time the couple finished drinks and dinner on a Friday evening, Sand, thanks to two tequila martinis, wine with his meal, and an evocative comment by Josephina, felt uncommonly self confident. Her comment came as they watched couples dancing to slow instrumental orchestra music. "Do you know what that kind of dancing is?" she asked with her customary smile. "It's a vertical imitation of a horizontal desire."

This was the same Josephina who had made the same comment to Zouch at their long-ago prom. She'd long forgotten all about Zouch, and, after four years of college, she had applied to four medical schools before she was finally accepted. But after her first year she dropped out with inadequate grades, then made her way through nursing school and graduated with a single aspiration: if she couldn't become a doctor, she could at least marry one and get rich.

In his plush Mercedes sedan, Sand drove Josephina from Reminiscence to his townhouse. At stop signs and red lights during the brief ride they kissed and touched each other. After champagne cocktails in the living room they rode the elevator upstairs and spent an hour in and near Sand's bed while music played and garish light shows danced on the ceiling and all four walls. Josephina performed uninhibited acts, things that no woman had ever done for Sand before. Resting afterwards, he told her he loved her, even though he knew he didn't. He asked her to marry him, and to his amazement she said yes.

Josephina had been friendly with many of the nurses Sand had been intimate with, and concluded that, as her husband, he would surely commit conspicuous adultery with at least one of her colleagues within months – possibly weeks – possibly days - of the wedding. Whenever it happened she would hire a lawyer. She understood that marrying Sand had been extraordinary luck. Now, if she did things correctly, she could soon acquire a small fortune simply by filing for divorce.

Six weeks and five days after the wedding, on a Friday morning, Sand, assisted by two nurses, carried out surgery on an obese middle-aged businessman. Sand had seduced one of the attending nurses in his office that week on a late Tuesday afternoon, and, late on Wednesday evening, had seduced the other on the back seat of his Mercedes parked outside her apartment.

News can travel quickly among hospital employees, and, during the Friday morning surgery, the two nurses, both embarrassed, while at the same time indignantly jealous, verbally abused one another over the anesthetized businessman. To escape his own embarrassment and their emotional dispute, Sand excused himself from the operating room before the patient's incision had been sutured by the flustered young doctor who had observed both the operation and the quarrelsome nurses. During surgery the usual sponges had been placed in the body cavity to absorb blood. The inserted sponges are routinely counted going into the body and counted again coming back out, but both the wrought up nurses and the young doctor missed the count. Six sponges went in, only five came out. Two hours later the patient's heart failed, and three days after that the hospital was cited in a lawsuit.

When the suit was adjudicated Sand's role in the operating room dispute between the nurses became public knowledge, and Josephina, citing serial adultery, filed for divorce and was awarded more money than she'd hoped for. Sand retired and settled in the woods, where he committed himself to making friends and consigned himself to celibacy forever.

PART TWO
THE CLEVER RACCOON

otro

Otro ran to Loot's against a headwind. Almost there, he stopped to kneel beside a creek and dip cupped hands to drink. Three fingerling trout nosing into the current over mottled gravel at midstream darted away when their water was disturbed. Just then the first drop of warm rain hit the back of Otro's neck. After drinking his fill he ran harder. By the time he sighted Eagle under the shelter in Loot's corral he was drenched. He climbed the outdoor steps three at a time and knocked four slow, evenly spaced times on the door.

"Get in here," Loot called.

Inside it was pleasantly warm with seasoned cedar smoldering in the woodstove. Loot was at work wearing a white, paint-smeared, old-fashioned long-sleeved man's shirt. As Otro crossed the room she stepped back from the easel, a brush in one hand and a lit joint in the other.

"You're just in time to offer an opinion," she said.

The black frame on the easel was heavy and square. On all four surfaces Loot had painted randomly spaced dime-sized pink circles combined with somewhat larger yellow and orange human hands. The yellow hands were clenched fists and the orange hands were cupped as if to receive a communion wafer.

"It's almost complete," she said. "Or it might *be* complete."

"Does it have a name?"

"Redemptive Reprisals."

"Meaning?"

"That should be obvious. It's bullshit that doesn't mean anything. I'll change the name if I can come up with something more pretentious that means even less."

"What could mean less than nothing?"

"Get out of those wet clothes."

As Otro undressed Loot tossed the remnant of her joint into the woodstove. He moved a wooden rocking chair next to the stove and hung his clothes over the back of the chair to dry.

"That white bandage makes your skin look darker," Loot said.

"I think Sand did a good job."

After they made love Otro lay on his back with Loot on her side and his arm around her with her head against his shoulder. Her hair smelled of soap. Rain drummed on the roof. As they talked, Otro gazed up at the heavy beams that crossed the pinewood ceiling.

"Sorry," Otro said, "I forgot the painting's name."

"Redemptive Reprisals, and that's the point. It's meant to be eminently forgettable."

"Why?"

"Why not?"

"Who's buying it?"

"A very rich freethinker who's in love with big words. I know a lot about him. He's barely thirty and already on his third marriage. The first two were expensive and I'd bet this one will be too. But in public he says all the right things and contributes to worthy causes. I think he feels guilty for being a rich scumbag and it's made him insecure. And he has to feel guilty for helping addict young people to worthless tech shit. Buying art instead of yachts and aircraft probably makes him feel better about himself."

"Where'd you find him?"

"He found me. To hell with him. His favorite pastime is talking about himself. I'm getting tired of what I do. I won't ever need any more money than I already have. All I need might be a little more revenge. So fuck selling crap to suckers."

"Watch your fucking language. But I know a good cave. Several in fact."

"That could work. But what's happening with you? What can I do?"

"I'm thinking Zouch will contact you soon."

"About you?"

"Sure."

"How bad is your trouble?"

"Bad enough."

"Tell me what I can do."

"I hate to ask but I will."

"Ask."

"Everybody knows about Zouch. When he has a chance he'll, as they say, hit on you. When he does it, be friendly."

"That *is* asking a lot. How friendly?"

"Nothing physical."

"I hope not. He's repellent."

"Most repellent men in power think they attract women because of the power. You're a lovely woman. So pretend you might like him. Just string him along. That's all."

"It'll be all but it won't be easy."

"You don't have to do it. But I have a feeling it might end up helping if you do. You might learn things."

"If he touches me or tries to I might vomit."

"Aim straight at him if you do."

"You're the only man who touches me."

Otro got up to feed a chunk of cedar into the woodstove and joined Loot back in bed.

"I have to watch out for White Lightnings. I had a run-in with three of them. They didn't come out of it well."

"I've never quite understood why they come out here."

"For a breath of fresh air. To look at us. To feel superior. For them it must be something like a visit to a freak show."

"Whatever their reasons are, you're making too many enemies."

"But I have friends too. And I have you."

"Ye.'"

Otro kissed Loot's forehead, then her cheek, then her mouth. "But I have to leave you soon – leave the neighborhood I mean."

"Where to?"

"Don't tell anybody what I'm telling you now. I'll ride Eagle to my place for what I need and then ride into the woods. I'll be safe, but I'll be close enough to know what's happening. The closer I am to home the safer I'm likely to be. I think I understand how Zouch's limited mind works. He's cowardly along with being stupid. If he was in trouble with somebody chasing him he'd travel as fast and far as he could. He'll most likely assume I reacted the same way he would. So I'll be all right. First I need to stir things up, create some diversions. Give people things to worry about. I'll be back to visit you soon. Do you have a small tarp to spare?"

"An old blue one, in the shed, folded up in the wheelbarrow. Eagle's bridle and reins are hung from a nail on the wall beside the door."

While Otro dressed in warm dry clothes next to the woodstove Loot buttoned up her paint-smeared shirt. With brush in hand she closed her left eye and tilted her head to the side to study the frame. "Two or three more clenched fists should do it," she said.

"Are you sure you want to give your work up?"

"I'll replace it with better work. I want to see if I can paint something and have it come out true. I'm ready to try that."

"Are there carrots for Eagle?"

"In the cupboard over the sink, the right-hand side."

There were carrots, onions, ears of corn, eggplants and jalapeno peppers. Enjoying the smell, Otro inhaled deeply. He chose three fat carrots.

After they kissed goodbye Otro walked out into the rain and jogged across the clearing. When Eagle saw him coming he nickered and then neighed.

Everything in the shed was neatly arranged. Stove wood was stacked high against one wall and leaning against the wood was a splitting axe with the handle wrapped from top to bottom in black tape. There were jars of preserved vegetables on a high shelf and three containers of green paint on a shelf below the vegetables. There were rakes and shovels leaning against a wall, and a workbench with a vise clamped to one end, and hammers, saws and drills lined up neatly across the top. Loot's well worn coffee-colored saddle straddled a sawhorse. Otro lifted Eagle's bridle and reins off the nail, took the tarp out of the wheelbarrow, and carried everything outside.

Eagle nickered again.

"Hola, amigo," Otro said. "Wie gehts?"

He rubbed Eagle's warm wet neck and then broke each carrot into four pieces and fed the pieces to him one by one. The horse lifted them off the palm of his hand with his rubbery lips. His chewing was loud, his breath warm. When Eagle finished the carrots Otro bridled him up, draped the tarp over his withers, and used a fence rail as a mounting block to swing up onto his back.

Otro rode at a walk up the hill and into the trees. As they moved through trees he talked to Eagle and rubbed his neck up and down with the palm of his hand. When they hit level ground Otro put him into an easy canter. The rain slackened and they made good time. Daylight was beginning to fade by the time they approached his dwelling from behind. The hard rain had muddied the creek.

loot

Mica – the word meant clever raccoon - was born into official destitution on South Dakota's Pine Ridge Reservation. A wealthy couple adopted her despite some initial misgivings and named her Michelle, but now, thanks to Otro, she had become Loot, and she preferred that name because, like so little in life, it was a good joke.

Her adoptive father was a senior vice president for a large fast food chain. Her mother collected rare books that she stored in a hermetic vault and never read. These were the parents who sent their Sioux daughter to prestigious preparatory schools and then to Stanford University.

Loot majored in history, which corroborated her belief that life on earth was fundamentally poignant. Virtually everything she had seen, experienced, read about, heard about and discussed suggested to her that various forms of legitimate happiness were possible for individuals willing to look for them and lucky enough to find them, but that, collectively, human beings ultimately failed to one degree or another at nearly everything they tried to do. The vast gulf between what life on earth could have been and what it had become continued to expand at an ever-accelerating rate. But it wasn't humanity's fault. Loot had come to believe that human genomes hadn't yet evolved to a level that enabled large groups of diverse individuals to cooperate to a degree that could make complex community life tolerable for everyone. In every area other than superficial creature comfort, tribal life had been superior. She found a few likeminded friends at Stanford who felt much the same way, and they ended up calling themselves The Jaded Jokesters. When any number of them gathered together to swim or hike, or smoke weed or drink wine, or just talk, they agreed that laughter was the only viable antidote for most forms of anguish. World history was a never-ending chronicle of too much pain, famine, pestilence, conflict, suffering, leading to inevitable death. America had been established by means of genocide and enslavement. Everywhere on earth, might made right. Greed had inevitably resulted in environmental devastation, and as a result the final act of human life might well be underway. Never-ending struggles between people, races, religions, ideas, with everything ending in death, should be properly regarded as a cosmic joke, not as something to whine about.

Loot's own joke - painting on empty frames - began by accident during her junior year. Her mentor was an art professor she had slept with occasionally, a middle-aged divorcee named Drac whose paintings had been briefly admired twenty years earlier, until a new fad had arrived, as it always does, in the world of allegedly high art. Drac had decided not to adjust his style and subject matter and had lived, painted and taught in relative obscurity ever since. When Loot told him she wanted to try to paint, he explained to her that talent was often of minor consequence. Yes, humanity had turned out legitimately great artists and would surely produce more. But in the modern commercial art world most people, a vast majority, liked what they were supposed to like, and took seriously any work they were told should be taken that way. What Loot should try to do to attract attention was something that had never been done before, at least not recently. By way of an extreme example of dubious yet successful originality, he told Loot about an Italian artist named Piero Manzoni. In 1961 Manzoni had produced 90 cans of his own excrement and called it "artist's shit," and in thirty grams per can it carried the same price tag as gold, and people bought it. So Loot should execute her own outrageous idea and hope it was somehow noticed and admired. Despite the fact that male artists had always been granted more respect and paid higher prices than females, an innovation in the form of a lovely young Native American's work would stand at least a passing chance at acknowledgement, respect, and money.

Drac came up with a plan: painting random objects that could be said to have obscure and therefore deep meanings on empty frames. If she did the paintings and he helped promote them, it could possibly earn both of them notoriety, with money to follow.

Loot recognized his idea as a joke she could play – her personal joke to mirror the joke of life itself - and she knew she would enjoy doing it even if no one ever noticed. She started off painting three extra-large frames supplied by Drac, who also suggested subjects and then titles for the finished works. A purple frame decorated with golden cremation urns became "Urned Umbrage." A yellow frame with rainbow-striped piles of dog feces (a subtle homage to Manzoni) was "Partisanship Squared," and a blue frame decorated with white donuts and greasy red sausages was "Stars and Stripes Evermore."

Thanks to Drac, the three frames were prominently exhibited in the spring student art show, along with explanatory paragraphs composed by Drac. He also submitted a review expanding on the content of the paragraphs to the art department's monthly blog. The empty space within the frames, he explained at length, clearly symbolized the emptiness of the so-called American Dream. The subject matter objectified on the frames constituted documented evidence that had helped obliterate the dream, not merely turning it into nothing, but showing how nothing – space – was inevitably surrounded by evil. Without space there could be no evil, and without evil there could be no space. The pure native blood of a female indigenous artist not only made such revelations possible, it infused them with incalculable value.

And the miracle happened.

A respected critic took Drac's gibberish seriously, attended the student show, and paid no attention to anyone's work except Loot's. He stood in front of her three frames, straight-faced, staring at them in turn, for nearly two hours.

The day after the critic left the show he visited Drac in his office – the two of them had occasionally met at social gatherings - and asked the professor to please expand farther on his interpretations of the painted frames. Drac, who had spent thousands of hours inventing ostentatious verbiage to make it through his classroom lectures, gladly obliged.

The critic, though he listened attentively, had no clear idea what Drac was talking about but managed to convince himself that it sounded right and therefore chose to believe it, whatever it was. That night he wrote an entry for his own blog, praising the frames and their nuanced and urbane meanings. The blog was read by tens of thousands, many of whom were wealthy, one of whom collected paintings that he both lent to museums and saved as investments. He arranged to visit the student show privately, and, as soon as he saw the painted frames, he wrote a $300,000 check for the three of them. Possibly because he owned fourteen labradoodles, the rainbow-striped dog feces – Partisanship Squared - was his favorite. Word of the sale spread quickly among other alleged connoisseurs, and Loot, to her astonishment, was well on her way to both notoriety and wealth. Drac's agreed upon sales commission was and would remain at twenty-five percent.

otro

Otro understood where, why and how wild creatures live and die, knowledge that allowed him to predict their most likely behavior. Though most human creatures are somewhat more complex than fish, birds and animals, he understood them nearly as well. That was how he saved himself.

There was no detectible sign of anybody on or near his property. During the half hour he waited and watched, with Eagle tethered behind him, a garbage truck and a light blue van with a roof-rack he recognized passed by on the road. The van belonged to a middle-aged man named Tarrant, who cultivated and sold high-quality black-market weed. Otro didn't know him well, or know anybody who knew him, but his product had won a reputation. The van slowed and stopped and parked on the roadside. Then Tarrant walked up Otro's driveway and onto the deck to knock on the door and stand there waiting. The sound of each hard knock reached Otro a split-second after Tarrant's fist hit the door. Tarrant waited a while and knocked again and waited again and finally called out:

"Are you in there? We need to talk! There's something we need to talk about soon! If you're there please open up!"

After a lengthy wait he called again: "Listen! It's important! Are you in there?"

He finally gave up and returned to his van and drove away.

tarrant

Marvin Tarrant, a homosexual Wharton Business School graduate, had been living in the mountains for years. Beforehand he'd enjoyed life as a top-level functionary at a large corporation. His misfortunes began soon after the company's longtime CEO retired and the board of directors chose a surreptitious homophobe named Schwarz Rauch to replace him.

Shortly after Rauch took over, while dining with his current mistress at a stylish Croatian restaurant, he happened to notice Tarrant at a corner booth across the room talking and laughing, and holding hands, with a handsome man. Rauch kept a close eye on the pair, and, soon enough, his suspicion was confirmed when Tarrant's companion leaned across the table and gave Tarrant a quick kiss on the cheek.

A half hour later, when the two gay men walked past Rauch's table on their way out, Tarrant smiled politely at his boss, and, instead of responding, Rauch, mouth clamped tightly shut, looked away to stare through narrowed eyes at his plate of skripavac.

"What's wrong?" the mistress asked.

"Why do you ask?"

"You look mad. Enraged in fact. I was under the impression I made you happy."

"Well then, why don't we discuss that? My impression is you'll be making me happy within the hour."

"If you lighten up, I'll do something special."

"Name your price, strumpet."

"A sapphire necklace."

"Deal!"

Despite cultural norms of the day among reasonable people, Rauch considered homosexual conduct depraved, and his devious campaign to see that Tarrant was terminated commenced immediately. As circumspect and calculating as any CEO, Rauch began sabotaging Tarrant's reputation by dropping cunningly negative hints about him at every opportunity. He also pressured carefully chosen subordinates into circulating rumors about his employee's substandard work. Before a month had passed, feigning regret, he had Tarrant fired by his immediate superior.

By the time the termination occurred Tarrant understood how and why it happened. He loathed ignorant homophobes at least as much as they loathed him, and even had a passing thought about murdering Rauch. But he knew it wasn't worth risking his own life to rid the world of a hopeless fool. Instead, he moved to the heart of a forest that offered ideal conditions for growing top-grade cannabis. He bought a large log house with outbuildings, searched hard and hired three skilled and trustworthy workers, and soon found a new boyfriend, an unconventional young man named Spurmeister.

Tarrant's business thrived, because he could under-cut the wholesale prices of legal weed while offering a superior product. Among his local customers were several White Lightnings, including O'brien. They were wealthy men who didn't need to save money on weed, and they liked the idea of being outlaws. On a cloudy afternoon in the recent past, with the three workers tending a grow and Tarrant at home with Spurmeister, O'brien, planning to make a quick purchase, had parked his Harley outside the log house.

Spurmeister opened the front door before O'brien had time to knock.

"Heard you coming," Spurmeister said. "Those fuckin' machines make some serious noise. C'mon in outa the rain, dude."

"All I need's five rolled joints, highest THC available, as usual."

"At your service," Tarrant answered from the kitchen.

O'brien stood waiting just inside the door as Tarrant crossed the living room and disappeared down a hallway. "Do you visit here often?" he asked Spurmeister.

"Yeah, dude, I do."

"Don't take it wrong," O'brien said, "but I have to ask you something of a personal question. I heard a rumor. So. Are you two faggots?"

Spurmeister shot O'brien twice, through the left lung and the heart, and, an instant before the first time he squeezed the trigger, he knew he'd never forget O'brien's bloodshot eyes widening in shock.

otro

After Tarrant's van passed out of sight Otro mounted Eagle and rode at a walk down the hill. The moment he opened his front door he knew that someone had been in his place. A book on the seat of a chair – *The Rise and Fall of the Third Reich* – was at least two inches out of place, and the bathroom door he'd left closed was slightly ajar. In the bathroom he discovered that a Patagonia shirt was missing from the dirty clothes hamper. Either Zouch or one of his deputies had likely taken the shirt for his scent.

Otro collected clean clothes, a long-bow and a quiver of hunting arrows, a serviceable knife, some hemp rope, a half-gallon plastic water jug, a tin cup, and a small box of waterproofed kitchen matches. He took elk jerky, smoked bass, dried fruit, coffee, and two large Granny Smith apples. Anything else he might need or want could be found, stolen or killed.

He decided to spend the night in his favorite cave – his home cave he called it - on the steep slope near the peak of the mountain behind his land. Years ago, while tracking a buck deer in October, he'd discovered the cave behind massive boulders scattered haphazardly at the base of a cliff.

Before mounting he quartered one of the apples and fed it to Eagle. The weather was cool and calm after the rain. On the way up the mountain a covey of quail flushed and just beyond the quail a bobcat darted out from underneath a deadfall tree. Otro assumed the bobcat had been stalking the birds. The cat scurried up-hill, looked back once, climbed the trunk of a tall white oak and ran out to the end of a slender limb. The limb bent under the animal's weight and the cat clung there at eye-level, staring intently at the approaching man and horse. When Eagle tensed and stopped, Otro urged him forward until he could have reached and touched the bobcat. It stared hard and Otro stared back and saw no fright in the animal's eyes and wondered what the animal saw in his.

"Have your proper life," he told the cat.

Ten yards beyond the oak Otro looked back and the cat was gone. As light faded fast the temperature dropped. He watered Eagle at a creek and filled his plastic jug. When they reached the cave just before dark Otro dismounted, tethered Eagle, and worked his way through the thick brush that grew among the scattered boulders, gathering sheltered twigs and branches that were dry enough to burn.

There was more space in the cool clean air of the cave than in his home. Everything remained just as it had been on his first visit. The floor was smooth gray stone and much of the stone roof was black with smoke from thousands of years of cooking fires. Among bits of charcoal left by fires were charred deer and rabbit bones. On the floor near the rear wall were three mortars, seven pestles, scattered obsidian fragments, two wooden bows backed with sinews, and a deer hide quiver of five arrows with bird points and hawk feather fletching. At the base of the rear wall lay the skeletons of two adults with the bones of a small child between them.

Otro piled kindling just inside the mouth of the cave, built a pyramid of larger branches over the kindling and lit his fire. He doubled up his tarp and spread it on the floor, then arranged his provisions.

Firelight illuminated the skeletons at the back of the cave. If he knew soon enough when it was his time to die Otro would do it here. He wondered how long it had been since smoke from the first fire in the cave touched the stone ceiling. He ate bass and fruit and brewed coffee and thought about it. Fatigued after a long day, he didn't think two tin cups of strong coffee would keep him awake. Somewhere nearby an owl hooted.

Stretched out on the tarp close to the fire, he dreamed of The Sea of Cortez, when he'd paddled his kayak over two blue whales cruising side by side a few feet beneath the surface of clear, calm water, their smooth skins glimmering under a bright sun. Blue whales were the largest animals on earth, grew to lengths of one hundred feet and lived as long as one hundred years, and their voices could be heard by other whales a hundred miles away. A blue whale calf drank as much as six hundred quarts of mother's milk per day. In his dream, Otro wondered how many years would pass before they became extinct.

>-<

Before dawn a howling coyote awakened Otro from deep sleep.

He rebuilt his fire over a bed of warm ashes and walked outside to urinate. Neither glad nor sorry the man was dead, he thought of the White Lightning O'brien, wondering who had killed him and why. After he finished he talked to Eagle and patted his neck. Back in the cave, he fed the fire and ate jerky and brewed coffee, and drank the coffee slowly while the tin cup warmed his hands.

"You're protected here," he told the skeletons. "You're safe. I'll leave soon but I might soon be back."

Otro left his supplies in the cave, walked Eagle to a nearby spring, mounted from a rock ledge and rode downhill. The eastern sky had lightened with clouds red as blood piled over dark, distant mountains. By the time Otro reached a promontory overlooking the long valley the clouds had faded to gray and there was light enough to see a long expanse of the empty road far below. He turned Eagle loose to graze and sat with his back against a rough-barked pine. He thought about the history of powerful rulers living high on hilltops where they could protect themselves from the people they ruled, and about how he was using a hilltop to observe people who wanted to rule him.

About two miles up the road was Mini's tavern. A mile beyond the tavern was a rich man's summer getaway mansion, the spacious grounds, including a nine-hole golf course, surrounded by razor wire and patrolled, day and night, by armed guards and attack dogs. Otro's place, and then Gold's, were well beyond that. Three miles down the road a slender plume of white smoke rising over dark trees marked where Loot lived. Otro guessed she might be up early to paint another hand or two for a rich fool.

In an hour's time only six vehicles passed along the road. The first was a high-end foreign sedan that could have belonged to either the rich man with the mansion or one of his relatives or guests. Next came a semi-truck and not long after that a black and gold sheriff's SUV speeding northward. It might have been driven by Dipple. By the time the lawman's car was out of sight another just like it sped by, red lights blinking. A minute later Otro heard gunshots, and then two large camouflage-colored vans appeared, traveling slowly, no more than ten yards apart, their occupants firing handguns and long guns out of open windows on both sides. They were teenage boys who frequently drove from town to lonely forests, usually on weekends, to shoot at any birds or animals they happened to see, or to discharge hundreds of rounds of ammunition into the trees for the joy of it. Otro had heard of a group that called themselves the Triple FFFers – Fusilladers For Fun.

He mounted up and rode to Gold's. By the time he arrived the sun had dimmed under a high blanket of wildfire smoke mixed with clouds. Gold's bright yellow dwelling sat between two wooded hills next to a pond stocked with bass and bluegills. The bass ate the bluegills and Gold ate the bass. Behind the pond was a vegetable garden next to a smaller garden for weed, both plots fenced against deer.

Otro reined up to watch from a distance. Gold's vehicle was parked beside the pond. Light showed through his kitchen window, and Otro saw Gold's shadow cross the window twice. He tethered Eagle and walked down and knocked twice at the door and after a pause opened the door and went in. Gold stood in his living room wearing baggy sweatpants, his muscular upper body bare. "I saw you coming," he said. "Guten Tag. Kaffee?"

"Danke. Bitte."

"Setz Dich."

Gold's barbell rack sat against the wall across the room. Otro took a chair at the oaken dining table next to the rack.

"I was doing some lifting and some writing along with it," Gold said.

He walked to the stove with his left-legged limp. Both legs bothered him and mornings were worst, and he smoked weed most mornings to mitigate the pain. Gold's open loose-leaf notebook lay on his desk, a ballpoint pen beside it. He wrote in longhand, as authors did long ago. Gold limped back to the table with two large mugs.

"Danke," Otro said.

"Bitte."

"Do you think Zouch might come out here sooner or later?"

"My gate's always locked and I doubt if he could make it here all the way from the road on foot even if he thought he had to. But he visited Mini's last night to ask if any of us knew where you were. All the regulars except Sand were there. Zouch had already checked at your place. We told him we had no idea where you were. He told us at least ten times that you're in serious trouble. 'A shit-load of trouble' is how he eloquently phrased it. He claims you resisted arrest and escaped. He called you a desperado. Is that a Spanish word?"

"No. The Spanish word would be forajido."

"I politely called Zouch a pendejo. I know what that means."

"How did he react?"

"He didn't know what it meant and nobody told him."

"Loot was there?"

"Zouch ended up taking her outside to talk, to question her. I told her she didn't have to submit to questioning outside or anywhere else if she didn't want to, but she seemed confident, said she didn't mind. And I told Zouch I'd hit him with a horrendous lawsuit if he mistreated you or any of your friends. Then I warned him that when the suit came up for trial I'd arrange for a change of venue to La Paz, Bolivia, where I have connections. He was enough of a pendejo – ein schwachsinniges Arschloch - to take me seriously."

"I expected he'd be harassing Loot. Did you talk to her afterwards?"

"She didn't come back inside. We heard her drive away."

"How long did they talk?"

"No more than ten, fifteen minutes. After Loot left Zouch came back to harass us a little more."

"Der Kaffee ist koestlich," Otro said.

"Bolivian. For some reason I had coffee in mind when I warned Zouch about the change of venue so I picked Bolivia. I also told him rumors were circulating that he planned to use illicit drug carrier money instead of his own to finance his campaign."

"Is it true?"

"I doubt it."

"Do you think Zouch can get elected?"

"I think it's possible."

"Thanks kindly for all your help. I've got Eagle outside. I'll ride to Loot's now."

"Mehr Kaffee zuerst?"

Otro felt guilty intruding on Gold's time but wanted more Bolivian coffee. "Bitte," he said. "Aber nur eine halbe Tasse."

Gold limped to the stove, poured coffee into both mugs and limped back with them.

"I apologize for interrupting your work."

"I needed a break. In fact I welcome it. I'll be better off because of it and the writing will be too."

"Tell me something. How strong are you? Mini told me she saw you squeeze a pair of pliers hard enough to snap the handles. Is it true?"

Half-smiling Gold looked away as if embarrassed.

"Yes, I can do that," he said.

"What could you do to a human being with strength like that?"

"If I wanted to – if I had to – I could use my hands to crush a human skull." He sipped coffee and looked at Otro over the rim of his mug. "I'm not sure I would though, even if I thought I should. I might mangle an arm or leg if necessary."

"Would you snap a pair of pliers for me? Only if you have an extra pair, and I'll reimburse you."

"You don't have to reimburse me. I must have a half-dozen useless pairs of pliers around the place. Why do you want me to do it?"

"Because it's hard to believe you can."

"Don't you believe it?"

"Yes… maybe… no, honestly I don't."

"I shouldn't do it just because I can. But all of us have our trivial vanities."

Gold limped across the kitchen again, opened a drawer underneath the sink, rooted around in it, and pulled out a pair of pliers. He limped back and offered them to Otro. "Check them out," he said.

"No, I don't have to check them out."

"I want you too. If I do something, even something I shouldn't do, I want it done properly."

Otro took the pliers. They were old and worn shiny with use, and heavy and strong. When he closed them tight there was less than an inch of space between the tips of the handles. He squeezed as hard as he could with both hands and then handed them back to Gold.

Gold took the pliers in his right hand. His forearm looked like brown leather stretched tightly over a network of bulging cables and wires. He sat smiling at Otro and closed the pliers and squeezed, and when one of the handles snapped he dropped the two pieces onto the tabletop.

Otro picked up the handle that had snapped off and saw that the break was perfectly clean. "Thank you," he said.

"Tell Loot to be careful with Zouch. He's known to have raped Mexican women he held in his jail. He locks them up for what he calls questioning. But he never asks them anything. Alejandro knows about that too."

Otro carried his empty mug to the sink.

"Take care," Gold said.

"Auf wiedersehen."

Otro cantered Eagle all the way to Loot's.

When he saw Loot from a distance she was hanging clothes on a line, and the wet wash danced in gusts of warm wind. When Loot saw Otro riding toward her she waved and smiled. He rode up and reined in, dismounted, and looped Eagle's reins around one of the stanchions supporting the clothesline. He kissed Loot until she laughingly pushed him away.

"I'm glad you're back," she said.

"I am too."

"I finished my frame this morning."

"I was wondering about that. You deserve some time off. A break, a vacation."

"I have a few more commissions to fill." Loot lifted a white brassiere from a wicker basket and used a single clothespin to hang it from the line. "A few more pieces of expensive crap and that'll be it."

"How many more?"

"Seven. No, no, eight. When I'm done with those I'll be ready to start over with some simple drawings, the kind Mini does. I doubt I'll ever be as good at it as she is, but I want to try."

"What's your next commission?"

Loot hung up a long-sleeved black blouse. "A geriatric pervert in Boston read about me in a magazine. I mean, this gentleman is *ancient*. Just short of his ninety-seventh birthday he married his seventh wife, a twenty-two year-old. I'm moving him up to the head of the line so he can pay me before he dies."

"A twenty-two-year-old could easily kill a man that old."

"A seventy-two-year-old could. Maybe eighty-two."

She hung up a pair of blue jeans faded nearly white.

"How did the pervert make his money?"

"He was the long-time CEO of a cigarette company. Or I guess they call themselves tobacco companies."

"How do you know so much about him?"

"My agent - Drac - checks out my clients' backgrounds for me. This one wants a frame representing - I should say symbolizing - his triumphant life. Suggestions?"

"Different colored dollar signs with arms and legs. Or wings."

"Too obvious. Too heavy-handed."

A permanently paint-stained white shirt emptied the clothes basket.

"Come on," Loot said.

They walked toward her dwelling, Otro balancing the empty basket on his head.

"Let's sit outside a while," Loot said. "Coffee?"

"I just had two mugs at Gold's."

"The Bolivian?"

"Yes."

Otro handed her the basket.

"I'll be back with mine," she said.

Otro sat on the fenced deck in one of four pinewood rocking chairs. There was a platform bird feeder attached to the deck railing and every morning Loot spread it with millet, dried corn and sunflower seeds. Jays, red-winged blackbirds, acorn woodpeckers, collared doves and sparrows came to the feeder. Loot believed that birds deserved to survive long after humans had managed to destroy themselves, and she wanted to help them along. When Otro sat down he frightened two Steller's jays away, and a few seconds after that an acorn woodpecker arrived. When Loot carried her coffee out the woodpecker left.

"Tell me about talking to Zouch," Otro said.

"The only thing that might be important is, he walked away to take a call while we were talking. Apparently he didn't think I could overhear him but I could. Nothing made complete sense but he mentioned Modoc Park more than once. Something's going to happen there."

"No idea what or when?"

"No idea. But something, soon. Today or tomorrow I'd guess."

The woodpecker glided from an oak limb back down to the feeder, cocked its head to look at the two nearby humans, then squawked twice before it began pecking up seeds.

"All Zouch wanted to talk about at first was you. He kept asking me how well I knew you."

"And?"

"When I told him we were close friends he laughed and said I could do better than you. I told him to go fuck himself."

"No you didn't."

"Yes I did."

"You were supposed to be nice to him."

"I half-smiled when I said it. I knew what I was doing."

"What were you doing?"

"Setting the scumbag up. Grooming the pendejo. And he knows I have connections to people who could hurt him. He isn't as dumb as he looks."

"I hope not."

"I wasn't in any danger but apologized anyway. I told him I was joking. He asked me if I knew where you were or where you'd be today, and if you'd ever talked about the dead White Lightning – what was his name?"

"O'brien."

"He asked me the same things over and over and I kept giving him the same answers, that unless you were with me I never knew where you were because you keep your plans, your life, to yourself. The whole time we talked after I told him to fuck himself I got progressively friendlier. Slow but sure. Finally I gave him my best fake friendly smile. I was testing out a theory I've believed in since my teenage years."

"What's that?"

"Women can be insecure about their looks but ugly men are even worse. A lot worse. Men like Zouch. He's a classic example. After a lifetime of angst, if some woman, any woman, can make a man like Zouch believe he actually has appeal, he's somehow able, temporarily, to ignore the proof he sees every time he looks into a mirror. I told Zouch that I cursed him in an attempt to protect myself, because I was attracted to him."

"And he believed it?"

"He did."

"Then he must as dumb as he looks."

"He's holding a political rally this weekend, his first big campaign rally, and he invited me to line up on the stage behind him. To show myself as one of his supporters. One thing I know for sure is, in his speech he won't talk about anything that really matters. He told me about a rumor that's going around – that some mean young man, Nate something or other, a hothead and an asshole troublemaker Zouch called him, will be running against him. The hothead's already given two or three speeches. Zouch'll want his speech to be about keeping scared people safe, protecting them from outsiders. That's been a standard political scam forever. Anyway, that's where you come in. You can bet he'll make a show of accusing you of murder."

"So you'll go onstage with him?"

"I didn't commit myself. But if I show up at his rally and somehow get lucky maybe we can make him pay. But forget him for now. Stay a while. Let's go inside."

"I want to but I have to go."

"Where?"

"I want to check out Modoc Park. Can I leave Eagle with you?"

"I remember something I read about Crazy Horse. Or maybe you told me about it. Remember? He said something like, 'If a man seeks the prize of his heart he doesn't stop to count horses.' I admire that sentiment."

"I only have one horse to count."

"One's enough if it's a good one. Come on inside. We won't be all that long."

"Ye.'"

crazy horse

Crazy Horse loved a woman named Black Buffalo, who was married to No Water and had borne him three children. Apparently attracted to Crazy Horse, Black Buffalo could have divorced No Water simply by placing his belongings outside their lodge, but for unknown reasons she didn't do it. Crazy Horse could have offered horses to No Water in exchange for his wife, but, always disdainful of formalities, he made no offer. Instead, while

No Water was absent on a hunt, Crazy Horse and Black Buffalo left the camp together.

When No Water returned and found his wife missing and learned she had gone somewhere with Crazy Horse he borrowed a pistol from a warrior named Bad Heart Bull, searched and finally found the lovers, and shot Crazy Horse in the face. Though the bullet broke Crazy Horse's jaw, he survived. Black Buffalo returned to her husband and, as a peace offering, No Water gave his best horse to Crazy Horse. When Black Buffalo's fourth child was born, a daughter, she was, like Crazy Horse, uncommonly light-skinned.

otro

With the shrouded sun low in the sky Otro sat cross-legged watching traffic from behind a stand of poison oak on a hillside high enough above the road so that he could see a long way in either direction. Dipple drove up the road and back down three times. A bright red pickup truck travelled south. Also heading south were two jeeps that likely carried hunters or fishermen. In the middle-distance a small flock of geese crossed the sky in a wavering V. Across the valley shifting sunlight transformed a single cumulus cloud from orange to pink.

Otro heard motorcycles long before they came into view. As White Lightnings passed in single file at high speed he counted twenty-three. All wore what looked to be a kind of uniform - black helmets and black jackets

- and soon after they disappeared around a bend up the road their motors revved loudly, then abruptly stopped.

Twenty minutes after the White Lightnings arrived at Modoc Park Otro was there. At a safe distance he watched them through buckbrush and pines. A short trail through the pines led from the parking lot to a grassy clearing with picnic tables and fire pits. A side-trail from the clearing gave access to an ancient wooden outhouse and just behind the outhouse was a small creek overgrown with blackberry vines.

The motorcycles were parked in a single long row in the lot and their riders had gathered at three of the picnic tables. There were six-packs of beer on the tables, and, as Otro watched, two men started a fire in one of the pits. He recognized the three men he'd debased sitting together at the table near the fire. An obese White Lightning from another table stood and waddled along the path toward the outhouse. A skinny White Lightning with a can of beer in his hand from the same table followed the fat one and passed the outhouse by. When he came to a break in the blackberries he stopped to urinate into the creek.

A red-bearded White Lightning with a beer in his hand climbed awkwardly onto a tabletop. "Listen up!" he yelled. "Sit yourselves down! Listen up! *All* you gentlemen, listen *up!* This is our chance, call it our golden opportunity, to have some authentic satisfaction! And do what's right in the process! Sheriff Zouch wants that lowlife killer! He wanted that murderous piece of trash – make it shit - *today.* But, unfortunately, we botched it.

To state it bluntly, we fucked up. The lowlife desperado got *us* instead. Got three of us anyway. Sorry to say it out loud, but he made us look like idiots! Well it's *our* turn now! We have help due to arrive soon. I'm talking bounty hunters. The genuine article. Zouch fixed it up somehow. Zouch's got some serious political activity scheduled this weekend and he wants that killer by then, has to have him, alive or dead, just like in the old-time cowboy movies many of us so dearly love. Three bounty hunters'll be with us right here, in an hour. An hour give or take a little. That lowlife misfit desperado murdered *O'brien!* Understand what I'm saying? Now we'll o*blit*erate him!"

As Redbeard finished his speech the fat and skinny White Lightnings rejoined the group, and a short man wearing a holstered weapon stood and tilted his head back to swig beer. After his last swallow he lowered his head and smiled, looked around at the crowd, then at Redbeard up on the table. "Well exactly how are we supposed to catch and or kill this desperado?" he asked.

"That's one reason the bounty hunters are on their way," Redbeard answered. "They're experienced. Experts. Trackers. Killers. Pros. So swill your brew 'til they show. And stoke that fire, gentlemen! It'll cool off out here soon!"

Many in the crowd laughed aloud when Redbeard hopped off the tabletop to stumble and nearly fall when he hit the ground.

Otro was near enough to hear the White Lightnings' conversations. A few talked about football games.

One of them bragged that his daughter was a high school cheerleader. Three of them talked about cowboy movies. Several talked about golf, and one bragged that he'd machine-gunned an elk, and another that he'd bought a new semi-automatic combat weapon and given his old one to his son on his twelfth birthday to formally make him a genuine American man.

As darkness fell and the air cooled the White Lightnings gathered between their blazing fire and a growing pile of empty beer cans. The bounty hunters arrived on schedule, in a clean white van with bright headlights, and a brighter searchlight mounted on the roof. They parked between the road and the line of motorcycles. The instant the headlights and searchlight were extinguished dogs in the van began to bark and howl.

Redbeard hurried to meet the three men in camouflage. He shook their hands, patted their backs, and walked with them back to the crowd by the fire.

As Otro made his quiet way toward the outhouse he dug through the forest duff to gather handfuls of dry sticks and leaves. When he opened the outhouse door he held his breath against the stench and piled kindling against a wall. Native people used fire for thousands of years to manage their land. Used correctly here it could confuse and frighten people. All it took was one match. The kindling flared, and the outhouse wood, seasoned for decades, flamed up instantly.

Otro hurried back through the dark to his hiding place.

Someone in the crowd yelled, "*Fire!*"

Another voice: "What the fuck?"

"Put it out!"

"Why?"

"They'll blame us!"

"Who gives a shit?"

"Put the fucker *out!*"

White Lightnings ran, walked and stumbled toward the outhouse.

Otro circled back to the parking lot. When he reached the bounty hunters' van three snarling hound dogs lunged at the windows, staining the glass with drool. They were tracking dogs and he knew for certain why his Patagonia shirt had been stolen. The dogs would eventually find his scent, and that would work to his advantage. After slashing the sidewalls of forty-six tires Otro watched the White Lightnings use their black leather jackets to beat at the orange flames burning the brush surrounding the outhouse.

"How'd the fucker *start?*"

"Get the fucker *out!*"

"How it *start?*"

"Get the fucker *out!*"

"Why the fuck are we doing this?"

"Fucking *do* it, man!"

>-◄

Otro averaged seven-minute miles, running the flats and downhills, jogging when he climbed. It took him more than two hours to reach the cave and would take the bounty hunters and hound dogs twice as long.

A hazy sky had cleared, and even after the long run the night air felt cold. Otro built a pyramid of kindling just inside the mouth of the cave. Later, when the bounty hunters arrived on the scene, he wanted them to spot the fire and then attempt to climb the steep hill to reach it.

He drank water and ate dried fruit, then used the hand-and-foot holds he knew to climb the nearly vertical cliff above the cave mouth. With both hands over the last ledge he stepped free of his foothold and pulled hard and swung himself up and over.

Facing Otro now was a long, uphill slope of land that led to the peak of the mountain. The trees of the slope were a mixture of oaks and lodgepole pines. As time passes limbs die and fall and so do whole dead trees, and here there was nearly as much wood on the forest floor as there was in the living forest. Otro dragged deadfall oaks downhill to the edge of the cliff. After a short rest he piled pine and fir limbs on top of the deadfall. When hundreds of limbs and dozens of trees composed the pile he searched and found a straight, sturdy oak limb to use as a lever.

Making his way carefully down the cliff took more time than it had to climb up. Otro lit his decoy fire at the cave mouth and waited and listened. Nearly half an hour had passed when he heard howling hounds in the distance. He added fuel to his fire.

With the fire blazing he climbed back up the cliff and sat directly above the cave, watching and listening. The bounty hunters made slow progress, their dogs howling and barking out ahead of them.

When Otro calculated the time to be right he wedged his oaken lever solidly underneath the collected pile of wood. By the time the bounty hunters reached the cave he could hear their voices clearly. The dogs had fallen silent.

"You think he's in there?"

"You in there, lowlife? Hey, Desperado!"

"Who else could have lit a fire way the fuck up here?"

"Spray it, man."

A long, loud burst of automatic weapon fire followed, and a few seconds later two short bursts, and then silence.

"Go on in."

"*You* go in."

"Hey, motherfucker! You dead in there?"

"Pour it in again!"

Another burst of fire.

"Fuck it! We'll *all* go in."

"You first."

Otro braced the lever against his right shoulder, counted off ten seconds to himself, and heaved hard. He felt the pile in front of him move and lift, and then heard trees and limbs crash-landing below. Shoulder pressed against the lever, bent at the waist, pushing with all his strength, he struggled forward. Limbs and trees fell even after he knew the cave mouth had to be sealed shut.

He heard the muffled voices.

"What the fuck?"

"Motherfucker!"

If the fire Otro had set in the cave spread to the fuel blocking the entrance smoke might asphyxiate the bounty hunters. Otherwise they'd be able to break limbs one at a time and move trees inches at a time to eventually escape.

"Where *is* he? Where *was* he?"

"Motherfucker!"

"Fucking smoke!"

The dogs howled.

the bounty boys

Tended to by servants and ignored by their parents, the three brothers, born a year apart, grew up eating calorie-ridden junk and, on most days, even school days, playing a video game that allowed them to become celestial bounty hunters delivering brutal justice to evil villains. Meanwhile, hopelessly spoiled and socially inept, they suffered relentless harassment at their church-affiliated private school. As time passed the level of verbal abuse gradually escalated, reaching its peak during their early teenage years.

Their parents owned and operated an international company that marketed audacious women's lingerie. Their most popular products included Invisible Lace Peekaboo Bras, Steamy Hot Panty Sets, Hot Night Crotchless Tedys, No Secret Transparent Nighties, and Lost in Endless Erotica Nighties.

At every opportunity smirking schoolgirls asked the brothers questions related to seductive garments:

"Wearing your crotchless pink underpants today?"

"Having some hot nights lately, shithead?"

"If I show you my Peekaboo Bra, will you show me yours?"

Boys tended toward fat jokes:

"You're so fucking fat lifeguards have to kick you off the beach to make room for the tide to come in."

"You're not really fat, you're just two feet too short."

"Suck in your flabby gut when you weigh yourself, asshole, that'll help."

At ages fifteen, sixteen and seventeen, during summer vacation, the brothers decided to drop out of school forever and dedicate themselves to becoming authentic bounty hunters, an occupation that they hoped would enable them to inflict pitiless payback on a world they knew to be heartless. Both parents surrendered to their sons' decision largely because it liberated them to focus more time on alleviating their boredom by squandering their wealth.

For five years, with their creature comforts supplied by servants, the brothers mastered the martial arts of Muay Thai and Sunshou and practiced with firearms, knives and swords. They read extensively about their centuries-old chosen profession. Historical bounty hunters they came to admire ranged from Charietto, a Germanic headhunter employed by the Romans in the third century AD, to the Dunn brothers in 19th century Oklahoma.

By this time their parents had convinced themselves that they shouldn't merely condone their sons' desire to battle evil, they should take pride in it. They established trust funds that guaranteed the boys munificent lifetime incomes. Because money would never be an issue, the brothers decided to utilize their expertise in rural areas, hiring themselves out to sometimes corrupt and often understaffed sheriffs. The relative absence of supervision and accountability in the wastelands would augment their opportunities to righteously inflict pain.

otro

Otro made his way down the backside of the mountain. If the bounty hunters and their dogs died he knew he'd feel sorry about the dogs. He came to a level clearing among big trees where elderberry bushes grew on the banks of a pond. He drank from the creek that fed the pond and then ate handfuls of bitter berries. He built a slow-burning fire and slept. What emerged in his dream was a world of lush green forests and clean air and water. Rivers ran free and every coastal stream teemed with runs of salmon and steelhead returning to spawn. High above the forests were massive flocks of migrating waterfowl. Bison roamed the grasslands and massive flights of passenger pigeons sometimes blocked the sun.

When Otro awakened before dawn he mourned for the world he'd dreamed. He rebuilt his fire, urinated and defecated, drank from the creek, ate more berries. In wild country Otro carried as much as he could of what he thought he might need. He searched the ground on his hands and knees around the elderberry bushes and soon found a cock blue grouse flank feather and used it to fashion a crude fly on a small barbless hook. He trimmed the feather and wrapped the hook-shank hackle fashion, starting at the bend and tying it off behind the eye.

Close to the pond the creek flowed fast and shallow over gravel. Upstream under tall trees the water deepened and slowed to form a pool. Otro tied the hook onto a short length of monofilament line, dropped it onto the surface of the pool and held it riffling on the surface near midstream. Three small trout rose one after another to hit the crudely fashioned fly but they were too small to hook themselves. After the small ones gave up a larger trout came up and held behind the fly for a few seconds and then made two quick passes at it but missed. It hooked itself on a third pass, and Otro lifted an eight-incher out of the water and smacked its head against a streamside rock. The trout quivered and died. Otro placed it atop the rock and dropped the fly onto the surface farther down the pool. The next trout he raised hooked itself on its first pass.

Otro gutted both fish, ran an elderberry stick through their gills and mouths, then roasted them over his fire. The slender bodies darkened and curved in the heat. He ate the trout with more berries, tossed the skeletons into the fire and washed himself with creek water.

There was morning light across the sky when Otro started down the mountain. The only sounds were his footfalls and a lone jay scolding from a tree. He jogged at a quick, steady pace and after an hour came to where the mountainside was strewn with slash and debris. Crossing the barren clear-cut he saw what loggers had left behind as artifacts: a dented metal lunchbox, a blue hardhat, the tattered remnants of a work shirt, soft drink and beer cans. At the bottom end of the clear-cut was the rutted dirt road that had given loggers access. Otro jogged along the road. There were oil cans and beer cans in the ditches. When he heard an approaching motor he concealed himself behind a patch of swordfern.

An old olive-drab jeep with its top down rounded a bend and climbed toward Otro and chugged slowly by. The three men in the vehicle wore orange hats and vests. Two of them were husky and the skinny one sitting in back held a rifle across his legs. Two more rifles leaned against the back seat pointing at the sky. The driver had a half-smoked cigar clamped in his mouth. The passenger beside him wore a thick white mustache and held a shiny silver whiskey flask between his legs with both hands.

Running down the road behind the jeep, Otro smelled exhaust fumes for the better part of an hour.

In early afternoon he arrived at Loot's. A thin trail of white smoke rose from her stovepipe chimney. Eagle grazed in the pole corral, and he saw Gold's vehicle parked beside the shed. He jogged down the hill and up the steps and crossed the deck and knocked four times.

"Get in here," Loot said.

"Otro!" Gold said.

"Gold!" Otro answered.

They were at the table. A half-empty brown beer bottle sat in front of Gold, and Loot held her customary coffee mug. They both looked troubled. Behind the table the black frame with clenched fists and open hands sat on an easel turned to catch the light.

"Pour some coffee," Loot said. "Or open a beer. Whatever you want. Sit down."

Otro took a mug from a kitchen shelf, poured coffee, and sat beside Loot across from Gold. "What's wrong?" he asked.

"They're after you," Loot said. "I mean, they're really after you. Seriously."

"I know, but they haven't caught me or even seen me. And won't. Has anybody been here?"

"Not yet."

"They've been to see Sand," Gold said.

"Zouch?"

"Zouch and another one."

"Most likely Dipple," Otro said.

"Do you think anybody saw you slashing tires at Modoc Park?" Gold asked.

"Nobody saw me."

"Are you sure?"

"Positive."

"Were the ones you saw armed?"

"At least a few of them were. But I've heard when they travel in crowds they tend to rely on strength of numbers to have their way."

"So far there's no legitimate proof that you've broken any law. We need to keep it that way. As things stand now, if they ever catch you and don't kill you and lock you in jail, I can get you out."

"After how long?"

"Hours. A day or two at the very most. What you should do is, go about your life as if nothing had happened, as if nothing out of the ordinary is going on around here or anywhere else. Nothing that concerns you. Go home and live your life. Yes, they'll take you in. Then I'll get you out."

Otro looked at Loot, who was looking at Gold. "No," he said.

"Listen to him," Loot said. "Please."

"How much do you know about Zouch?" Otro asked Gold.

"What I know for certain is that he's wealthy, stupid, sadistic and insecure. I suppose we all know that. Those qualities add up to a man who can't resist abusing his power. He might well have already killed you if he didn't know who I was. What I represent. He might have killed me if he didn't know about the people I know. The point is, I explained things to him in language even he could understand. You have to either let Zouch take you in, and trust me to get you out, or else run away, far away, and stay away unless – until - the situation changes. It's not likely, but whoever killed O'brien could turn up. Or Zouch could win his election, or lose it, and forget about you and O'brien both. Right now all you represent to Zouch is a chance for him to win some votes."

Otro thought Gold might be overestimating his influence on Zouch, and underestimating Zouch's level of ignorance and sadism. He decided to lie. "All right," he said. "I'll leave the area for a while. On Eagle I can easily cover fifty miles a day. I'll hunt and fish. I'll have time to think things through. What day is it?"

"Tuesday," Gold said.

"All right. I'll leave the vicinity. I'll be back in exactly two weeks." He took Loot's strong brown hand and held it. "I'll mark the days off carefully."

"There's bad weather coming soon," Gold said. "Rain and wind. Lots of rain and hard wind. Floods for sure."

"I'll be safe. I can handle weather. I'll be back here at this table two weeks from today. We'll see where things stand then."

"Odds are things will be the same." Gold said. "Or close to it. Or worse."

"We'll wait and see," Otro said. "I'll give myself until then."

Gold nodded his head and raised his bottle and drained the beer in three swallows. He slowly lowered the empty bottle to the tabletop. "It's your decision," he said. "I'll respect that. I'll leave now so you two can have some privacy." He pushed up from the table and limped across the room and out the door. Loot and Otro heard him walk across the deck and slowly down the stairs and then they heard him drive away.

"Where will you go?" Loot said.

"There's plenty of country. I'll go far enough. I know how to hide."

"I don't believe you."

"Don't believe what?"

"That you're going far away."

"Why don't you believe it?"

"I know you. Don't you think I know you'll stay around here?"

"All you need to know is what I told you. That way if anybody asks about me, that's all you can say. It's all you can say because it's all you know. I'll be thinking about you. Every day. Every hour. You know that too, don't you?"

Loot stood on the deck to watch Otro cross the meadow toward the corral. When he opened the gate Eagle was there to meet him. After Otro mounted he turned to wave. Loot, now wrapped in a Sioux blanket, waving back, stood in silhouette against an orange sky.

➤•◄

Alejandro's dwelling sat at the base of a forested hill at the end of a rutted dirt road. The windows on either side of the front door showed yellow lantern light through drawn curtains. Three old pick-up trucks were parked outside. As he looped his reins over a tree branch, Otro heard talk and laughter.

Then the door opened and Alejandro stepped outside. "Adelante," he said. "I heard you out here. Mini's here and my cousin and some friends."

Otro followed Alejandro through the door and saw seven people sitting in chairs around two small tables pushed together near the middle of the room. The tables were ringed with beer bottles and shot glasses, with an uncorked less-than-half-full bottle of tequila in the middle of it all.

Mini smiled at Otro and Alejandro's cousin Salvador brought Otro a folding chair. Alejandro reached into a beer cooler and brought out a wet green bottle of Dos Equis.

"Gracias," Otro said.

"Por nada. I hoped you might come here."

"Nobody at the tavern tonight?"

"I closed it for the time being," Mini answered. "Zouch keeps stopping by. Last night when I wouldn't answer his questions about you he called me names and threatened me."

"What did you do?"

"Called him a name he couldn't understand back."

"What name?"

"Cara de Puerco. Pig face."

Everyone laughed.

"Appropriate choice," Otro said. "Please, tell me what you know," he said to Alejandro.

In Spanish Alejandro told Otro that, besides bounty hunters, Zouch had called in volunteer off-duty deputies from other towns to help in the search. The White Lightnings were back on their motorcycles. They would patrol the roads while the bounty hunters with their dogs searched the woods. Zouch bragged that one way or another he'd capture or kill the desperado within days.

Otro was glad to learn that the dogs were alive.

"Que haras?" Alejandro said. "What will you do?"

Otro, who knew that it was possible to lie in the interests of truth, kept lying. "I'll disappear for a while. I'll go far away where nobody can find me."

"Cuan lejos? Donde?"

"I shouldn't tell you where. If anybody asks you if you know where I am, tell them the truth. No lo se. You don't know."

"Si. Clara. Bueno."

Looking in turn at the brown faces around the tables, Otro saw that some of them knew he was lying.

"Tequila?" Mini asked. "Uno pequeno?"

"Gracias, no. Mas cerveza por favor."

Alejandro reached into the cooler again.

They sat and talked. Mini and Otro drank beer while the other men sipped tequila. Alejandro told Otro that Gold had given him twice what the transmission repair had been worth, and when he'd tried to return the money Gold refused to take it. Salvador talked about an important soccer match in Mexico City. Two of the friends argued excitedly about the soccer match and ended up laughing together. The third friend asked Otro about his head wound.

"Un idiota lo hizo," Alejandro said.

"Idiota?"

"Si. Un pendejo grande."

"Cara de Puerco," Otro said. "Mi cabeza esta bien. No problema."

The third friend told what he'd seen that afternoon in the Mexican restaurant in town. The Comida Celestial offered an open challenge. Anyone who ordered a platter of thirty chorizo tacos got them for free if he could finish them in thirty minutes. At lunchtime a skinny Mexican boy in worn clothes had walked into the restaurant to accept the challenge. No one watching believed he could do it, but he swallowed down the last bite of the last taco with more than two minutes to spare. When the restaurant crowd stood and applauded and cheered the boy smiled shyly and bowed at the waist. After the taco story Mini told a dirty joke in Spanish about a one-legged man and a skinny woman locked up together in a closet. Everybody laughed. Otro took half an hour finishing his second beer. Alejandro came outside when he left. He squinted through the night at Eagle. "Caballo hermosa," he said.

"Hermosa y fuerte tambien."

They heard a short burst of quiet laughter from inside as they shook hands.

"Adios, amigo," Alejandro said.

"Adios, hermano."

Otro mounted and rode off through the trees. He soon crossed a wide creek and then came to a burned over stretch of forest. Upright trees were charred black and a thick layer of ash coated the forest floor. Weeds and brush and a few seedlings had penetrated the ash and more new life would follow slowly, year by year.

After two miles of devastation Otro reached a sparse forest of lodgepole pine. Another mile into the pines he saw the glow of fire. He gave the whistle and Otro's old friend Bull whistled back as Eagle continued through the trees. These days the Forbearing Dropouts were camped in a stand of scraggly pines close to a clean creek. Yurts - gifts that Bull had provided - were set on wooden platforms and loosely grouped among the trees. Tonight more than half of them showed golden lantern light through their translucent walls. At the center of everything was a stone-lined fire pit, and as he led Eagle toward the fire various Dropouts greeted him.

"Otro!"

"Crystal!" Otro said.

"Otro!"

"Luke!"

"Otro!"

"Blinker!"

"Otro!"

"Bull!"

Bull sat on a fallen log with Blinker and a woman he introduced as Ashes, who smiled up at Otro. She wore a green hooded sweatshirt and faded jeans and her thick black hair was cropped close. Blinker, brown-haired and skinny, in baggy pants and a green sweatshirt, wore a black leather pirate patch over his left eye.

blinker

His parents grew russet potatoes on a farmland homestead that had been in the family for five generations. Ever-warming winter temperatures had reduced winter snowpacks. With spring runoffs depleted, reservoirs that supplied irrigation water were often drained dry by the Fourth of July, by Labor Day at the latest. Meager crops became the best they could hope for, and financial aid granted to farmers by the state and federal governments was barely enough to keep them alive.

Despite their hardships, and also because of them, Blinker's parents had done their best to instill their son with generational family values. They taught him to hate people of color, abortions, vaccinations, socialists, pornography, and anti-gun radicals. They often spoke to him about their newly found deliverance - the Sect of Theseus and its leader, a self-proclaimed man-god who called himself Brother Brawn. When Blinker was sixteen years old the parents judged him mature enough to experience what Brother Brawn called an Admonition. He presented his Admonitions up and down the rural Northwest, traveling state to state and county to county in a rejuvenated army surplus helicopter.

Brother Brawn was a handsome middle-aged man, a classic American grifter with no known origin who understood how to exploit his time, his place, and his gullible patrons. On the night Blinker saw him perform he appeared in a large and dilapidated red barn wearing overalls underneath a white satin robe. With a crowd of citizens seated on metal folding chairs, Brother Brawn, standing tall and rigid as a fencepost, delivered a variation of his familiar message from the bed of a monster pickup truck, arms out to his sides as if he'd been crucified or might be about to take flight southward for the winter. He spoke beseechingly, and quietly, which compelled his audience to listen closely:

"Hear this, please, listen to me. Hear me." After stroking his white robe with his right hand, he resumed his crucifixion posture. "Think white," he began. "As you know full well, our god, Theseus, the only god there ever was or ever will be, has compassionately warned the world. In Theseus' all-knowing goodness, he has forewarned us, because he wants us to circumvent his wrath. The dazzling day of eternal salvation is close at hand. Should pure members of Theseus' flock suffer for the falsehoods of mankind's collusion? Floods? Fires? Pollution? Disease? Violence? These are no more and surely no less than celestial warnings launched to us directly by Theseus himself. Hear me now. Listen. I am Theseus' emissary, the humble human chosen to converse with those among us who deserve salvation." Glancing toward the ceiling of the barn, he stroked his white robe again, this time with his left hand. "I have no idea why I happened to be chosen, but I was, and, as always, I offer my subservient thanks for the sanctified honor. Listen, please, I beseech you. Here we are, trapped on a planet that constitutes an insignificant speck in the vastness of endless space. The truth revealed to me by Theseus is that our inconsequential speck was chosen to winnow out unworthies. Here then is Theseus' absolute truth. An armada of celestial spacecraft will arrive to carry us, the worthy – think white - far, far away. But where to? To a perfect planet, to a new earth, but it will not be an earth, it will be a paradise. The only paradise ever to have been or ever to be. Theseus will reveal to me the day, the time, the place when a grand armada will come for us, and when he informs me I'll inform you, and we'll depart together and then arrive together, in a new unearthly paradise. And there we will dwell forever."

Toward the Admonition's end, Brother Brawn's voice gradually rose. "The sinners who are left behind? As planned from the beginning of time, if indeed time has a beginning, sinners will be abandoned on this hopeless orb, this useless speck. That is Theseus' chaste objective. So you must heed his all-knowing, merciful warnings. As he has recently informed me, the time could be later this week, or this month, or later this year. Or even later than that. Whenever it is, accept his inducement to us, the righteous. All sinners will be shunned and therefore experience the brutal reality of what heathen scientists have chosen to call climate change. Climate change? A million times, a billion times no! Climate revelation – a trillion times yes! Hear me now, listen to me, please. This vile earth is our testing ground, our final examination. Here on this substandard and doomed planet, erroneous people will be left behind to suffer in Hades forever." Once again, Brother Brawn stroked his robe, this time with both hands. "Think white forever. Think T A P, which I'll now explain."

A popular country music song – "Count Me Out and Then Let Me Back In," sung by Sammy Toogood - sounded softly from a nearby vacant horse stall.

Now Brother Brawn's voice boomed. "Thank you for coming here to be with me tonight. Heed me now! Heed me! Long ago people talked about UFOs – Unidentified Flying Objects. Then they talked about UAPs

– Unidentified Aerial Phenomena. What the flying objects were, and are, is Theseus observing us from his celestial spacecrafts, and judging us in the process, and promising those of us found worthy an eternal life with T A P – Theseus At Paradise! Brother Power will greet you at the portal with our blessed receptacle, where you may discard your soon-to-be worthless lucre, your worthless money. It may well be that you have no great amount of money. But understand. That doesn't matter. Any amount of money is worthless. Soon, when Theseus deems the time to be perfect, his gift of an eternal life in a perfect place awaits us. To celebrate this, Brother Power and I will ignite your superfluous money - call it lucre - and the radiant flames will be seen and loved by Theseus, and the smoke produced by the radiant fire will hasten the death of earth and bring you closer to liberation – think white - think deliverance – think T A P!"

A smiling, sweating Brother Brawn finally dropped his arms to his sides.

➤•◄

Blinker's closest friend, a boy known as Whip, also attended the Admonition with his parents that night. The next morning the two boys met in a public park and quickly reached a solid agreement: their parents were fucking idiots and Brother Brawn was a lying sack of shit. They'd heard more than once from reliable sources that all he really cared about was getting blow jobs.

After two weeks of preparation the boys left home with backpacks, sturdy boots, camping gear, provisions and determination, and made their way to a distant range of mountains.

ashes

Ashes, born Ashley Martin, grew up in a family that had long been involved in idiotic right-wing politics. Both her quiet mother's and boisterous father's heroine was mid-20th century American novelist Ayn Rand, whose quotes, in gold-plated frames, were displayed in every room in the Martin household. One per wall, these four hung in Ashley's bedroom:

> *Force and mind are opposites; morality ends where a gun begins.*
>
> *Wealth is the product of man's capacity to think.*
>
> *Run for your life from any man who tells you that money is evil.*
>
> *Money is the barometer of a society's virtue.*

At age 17, at the urging of her father, who presided over a nationwide chain of savings and loan companies, Ashley read Rand's most popular novels, *The Fountainhead* and *Atlas Shrugged*. She judged the writing overblown and awkward, the characters under-developed, the themes repulsive. But she understood that, young as she was, no one, least of all her father, would take her opinions seriously. If she told him what she thought at the dinner table, the only place he ever listened to anybody, he would likely laugh at her, and, if he'd downed his customary quantity of evening martinis, he'd pound on the table and scream insults at her after laughing. So, correctly guessing that before a week had passed he'd forget about giving her Rand's novels to read, she kept her opinions to herself.

But her curiosity led her to research Ayn Rand, and what she learned confirmed her opinions. The author argued that self-interest was virtuous and altruism was destructive. She was an adulteress, fittingly married to an adulterer, and her personal relationships were more often than not disgraceful. A hopeless drunkard and a heavy smoker, she was eventually stricken with lung cancer. Despite having spent a lifetime denouncing government intervention, she enrolled in both Social Security and Medicare. At Rand's 1982 funeral the centerpiece was a six-foot tall floral arrangement in the shape of a dollar sign. The flowery dollar sign was the vulgar detail that turned Ashley Martin into Ashes.

otro

"So long, Blinker," Bull said. "Back soon, Ashes."

Bull and Otro walked away together with Eagle trailing behind.

"I know all about Zouch," Bull said.

"Already?"

"Everybody's heard about it."

After they passed out of firelight Bull stopped to urinate against a tree trunk. They came out of the trees into a clearing and stopped to talk while Eagle grazed.

"Been talking about you," Bull said. "Been talking about you two days now. Fact is, a minute or two before you gave the whistle Blinker asked me if you're sure enough an Indian. Said he heard someplace you were out of some Mexican tribe famous for running long distances. I mean *crazy* distances. Hundred fucking miles, sometimes maybe even more."

"The Tarahumara," Otro said, "from the Copper Canyon. Barranca del Cobre."

"You one of them dudes for real?"

"Does it matter? I could be from Egypt, Tibet, South America. What matters now is I'm you and you're me. Here we are."

Laughing hard, Bull threw his head back. "Yes!" he said. "I dig it!"

"Now I need your help."

"You got it. What kind?"

"I need you to stick with me for a while."

"Starting when?"

"Tomorrow morning."

"You got it."

"You ride Eagle and I'll travel afoot. We'll locate some of the people after me. We'll deal with them whenever and however we can. I won't wait for them to make things happen. I'll make things happen. We will."

"To Zouch and his stooges?"

"And some out-of-town cops and bounty hunters."

"Bounty hunters? How many?"

"Three that I know of."

"You can count on me, brother."

"Bad things might happen. Almost certainly they will."

"Don't be naïve, man. Not you. Bad things *always* happen. Hey. Gettin' chilly out here. Let's warm up back by the fire."

Eagle followed them back. Blinker and Ashes were gone from the log. Lantern light showed through the walls of most of the yurts. Bull took a thick limb from the wood pile, snapped it over his thigh, and then broke the two halves the same way. Sparks flew when he tossed fuel onto the flames. They watched the new wood catch and burn and sat on the log and talked in the warmth. Otro told Bull most of what had happened so far and explained as best he could why he had no way of knowing what might happen next.

"You know I can fight," Bull said. "Done plenty of it, mostly for the wrong reasons. This sounds right though. I can make up for some past sins. Maybe it's what I need."

"It's been a long day. Tomorrow might be longer."

"Need anything?"

"I'm good out here. Do you have a steady woman?"

"Ashes shares my yurt."

"Go on then."

Before he left to join Ashes, Bull fed more wood to the fire.

For a long while Otro lay awake. As he weighed his options he heard sounds of muffled voices coming from the yurts. One by one, the lanterns were extinguished.

He heard sounds of sex, and after everyone fell silent he heard Eagle cropping grass.

➤·◄

In lantern light Otro and Bull ate a breakfast of jerked venison, dried pears and double-strong coffee. Setting out from the encampment, the only sound was loud snoring coming from a nearby yurt.

They stationed themselves on a hill overlooking the intersection of two roads. A nearly full moon showed dimly through a hazy eastern sky. They hadn't been there long when Dipple drove out from town at high speed with someone small in the passenger's seat beside him. Following Dipple were six White Lightnings on Harleys that showed no lights. When the motorcade turned right at the intersection Otro assumed they were headed for Mini's.

"Do you know much about the White Lightnings?" he asked Bull.

"I know they're racist motherfuckers. That they come out here to hassle us."

Otro and Bull made provisional plans with contingencies that included attacks, diversions and retreats. As they talked, Otro watched a skein of geese passing so high overhead that they looked like a wavering length of string moving across the sky. He realized that, wherever it had come from, yesterday's wildfire smoke was gone. Then, when he saw Dipple driving back alone, he told Bull he thought the racist motherfuckers were at Mini's

Tavern, or would be soon. "I feel confident today," he said.

"Me too," Bull answered.

"And I don't think they do," Otro said.

Otro ran to Mini's with Bull riding behind him on Eagle.

Bull stayed with the horse a safe distance behind the tavern while Otro made a careful reconnaissance. In the parking lot a line of Harleys leaned on their kickstands. Otro found the storage room at the back of the tavern unlocked. He stood inside among cases of beer and whiskey, empty buckets and mops and brooms. Two walls of the room were covered with Mini's drawings, held there with silver thumbtacks. The portraits of people he knew seemed at least as alive as the people themselves. Loot was there. Alejandro. Gold. Sand. Between Gold and Sand was a familiar face that Otro couldn't place and seconds passed before he realized it was his face. Loot's was the portrait he studied. Delineated in simple lines and minimal shading, she was smart, funny, happy and sad, all at once.

Otro looked at Loot and loved her and listened while the White Lightnings, a few feet away on the other side of a thin wall, talked among themselves and insulted Mini as she served them. Apparently they had made the tavern a headquarters for bounty hunters and cops. While White Lightnings patrolled the roads the bounty hunters would search the country with their dogs. The sooner the better, Zouch wanted Otro captured or dead.

"Anybody know where the fucker's from?"

"Nobody knows. Who gives a fuck about that?"

"Well how long's he been in these parts?"

"Who knows?"

"Too long. And he definitely doesn't belong."

"That's the truth!"

"Well he's been here a while. He knows the country. Got to admit that."

"One thing for sure is he's crazy. *Runs* everywhere. *Every*where."

"Doesn't even wear *shoes!*"

"That's impossible."

"No it's not. No *shoes* even."

"He's a true fuckin' savage then."

"A desperado, right?"

"Bring more beer here. What's your name, bitch?"

"Mini."

"Bring more beer!"

"Maybe he's fifty miles from here."

"Or five fuckin' hundred."

"I said beer, bitch!"

"Yeah, sure, and maybe he's not."

Otro ran back to Bull. They revised their plans. Bull would knock on the door, enter the tavern and claim to hate Otro, and volunteer, even though he wasn't white, to join up with the White Lightnings. None of them would know who he was, and despite the fact that he was black they'd accept the aid of a powerful collaborator.

>-<

165

Bull circled the building and Otro returned to the storage room. As Otro emptied a bottle of whiskey onto the floor he heard Bull pounding on the tavern's front door.

"Holy shit!" came a voice. "Who the fuck are you?"

"A friend," said Bull. "Your friend, I hope to be. I know who you're after and I want to help."

"For real?"

"You heard me."

"Look at the *size* of this dude."

"Get in here, man!"

Otro ran to the parking lot and saw that the front tires of all the Harleys were flat. He wondered if Dipple had been there ahead of him to do it. He flipped the closest cycle upside down to release gasoline into the empty whiskey bottle and then returned to the storage room to listen. They were still talking about him.

"The way it ended up was, we chased that sorry barefoot bastard all the way up a mountain."

"But couldn't catch him?" Bull said.

"Should've but we never did."

"You weren't armed?"

"No."

"Next time'll be different," said another voice.

"More beer here!"

Otro ran back to Eagle, mounted up, cantered through trees to the edge of town, and tethered Eagle near Cadaver Creek. No one was in sight in either direction along the road. Carrying the whiskey bottle full of gasoline, changing hands every mile or so, he ran hard to the county jail. Dipple's vehicle was in the lot and

Zouch's wasn't. Otro decided that Dipple had flattened the Harley tires. He crossed the road and hurried along the deserted alley behind the pawn shop and poured gasoline onto the splintery wood at the base of the rear wall. When he applied a match the gas made a small explosion. As flames began to spread he hurried back across the road to watch from behind the hedgerow that bordered the jail. Brownish smoke rose from behind the pawn shop and orange flames followed. Two men ran out the front door screaming *Fire* and one of them reached into a parked car to honk the horn. A skinny man in a white apron walked out of the pizza joint and saw the fire and ran back in.

Dipple hurried out of the jail and sprinted toward the fire, and by the time he'd crossed the road Otro was into the jail. As he jogged down the hallway the three Guatemalans and the scrawny white inmate stood to look at him.

"Que pasa?" one of the Guatemalans yelled.

"Vuelvo enseguda," Otro answered. "I'll be back."

From the pegboard beside the door in Zouch's office he took Dipple's vehicle keys and the antique key he was certain would open the cells.

When Otro unlocked his cell and pulled the door open the white man backed himself against the wall underneath the barred window and shook his head and held out both trembling hands as if to fend Otro off. "No no no no no!" he said. "You ain't foolin' me!"

"You're free if you choose to be," Otro said. "Quieres salir?" he asked the Guatemalans.

"Si. La imigracion nos quiere."

He unlocked their cells and they followed him down the hallway and outside.

"Quien eres tu?" one of them asked.

"Tu amigo. Ven comigo. Puedes conducer?"

"Si."

Otro handed him Dipple's vehicle keys and suggested he drive to wherever their nearest friend was and plan their escape from there.

"Gracias!"

"Prisa!"

"Gracias! Si!"

The Guatemalans piled into Dipple's SUV and Jesus drove them away.

By then several men were fighting the pawn shop fire. Dipple used a garden hose and three men ran back and forth from the pizza joint with aluminum buckets sloshing water.

Otro mounted up and crossed Cadaver Creek and rode through the trees to Modoc Park, and, as he'd anticipated, found it deserted. Beer cans and cigarette butts were strewn where the White Lightnings had gathered. Wisps of smoke rose from the smoldering pile of ashes that had been the outhouse.

He waited there for Bull.

bull

At age sixteen Leroy stood six-feet-five-and-a-half inches tall and weighed 260 solid pounds. That was the year football teammates gave him the nickname Bull. At eighteen he'd grown to six-eight and weighed 280. A defensive lineman, he was offered dozens of scholarships by major universities but, to the dismay of coaches across the country, he turned them all down. He explained to disbelieving family and friends that he was sick of taking orders from coaches and tired of having referees blow whistles in his ears.

Instead of playing football Bull left home and found a job installing expensive tombstones in exclusive cemeteries for a marble and granite company. The tombstones were composed of volcanic rock that weighed more than 150 pounds per cubic foot. So long as Bull did his work - and he did it well - no one bothered him. By the time he quit that job after three years he'd put on an additional 18 pounds of upper-body muscle.

Next he became a rodeo clown wearing baggy clothes and a woman's bonnet whose function was to protect cowboys thrown from Brahma bulls. He felt that his nickname made the job appropriate. Whenever a rider went down, Bull distracted the animal to give the man time to escape. The dangerous times were when an injured cowboy lay in the ring immobilized and Bull had to station himself between the enraged bull and the injured man. In the last rodeo he worked an exceptionally huge white Brahma charged Bull and slammed into his chest and sent him sprawling, and then commenced to gore the fallen rider. Bull came off the ground, sprinted up from behind, jumped onto the Brahma's back, clasped his hands together underneath the massive throat, rolled sideways, took the animal down, and strangled it to death. The notoriety of the exploit led to Bull's mixed martial arts cage fighting career.

After brief training in boxing, wrestling and Brazilian Jiu-Jitsu, and growing wild hair and a bushy beard, he won bouts easily wherever he fought. Most of his battles ended in less than thirty seconds. He specialized in double-leg takedowns, ground-and-pound and guillotine chokes. Promoters soon understood that MMA fans wanted more than half a minute of intense and bloody violence for their money, so they insisted that Bull allow his fights to last longer. He steadfastly refused, and with enough money saved to keep him solvent for the foreseeable future he quit the game, shaved off his hair and beard, found the Forbearing Dropouts and joined them.

otro

Otro watched occasional vehicles speed toward town. One of them was Fergy's truck. Not far behind it were two vans carrying teenage boys, their haphazard gunfire echoing off distant hills. Soon after the vans were gone and the gunshots had faded Mini's van turned into Modoc Park.

Otro rode Eagle down a hill and across the road to join Mini and Bull.

"Mini!"

"Otro!"

"Bull!"

"Otro!"

Bull's shirt was torn and smears of dried blood nearly as dark as his skin showed on the knuckles of both hands.

"We can stay out of sight behind the blackberries over where the outhouse used to be," Otro said.

They stood in the sun next to blackberry vines, well out of sight from the road. Otro asked Bull about the tavern.

"I took my opportunity to resolve things."

"He sure did," Mini said with a small smile.

"The time seemed right," Bull said. "My instincts kicked in."

"Did you kill anybody?"

"Oh no. I held back. They were all breathing when I left." He raised his huge right fist and looked at it, and opened and closed it and looked again. To Otro the fist looked like the head of a black sledgehammer. "No broken bones," Bull said. "Not my bones I should say. Hey, Mini, you can tell Otro about it while I wash up in the creek."

Bull went to the creek and Mini explained. The White Lightnings swallowed all his lies. Bull had told them he'd spent time in jail after Otro had testified against him in court. He told them that Otro's testimony had been lies, and now he finally had his chance for revenge. Taking full advantage of a situation that gave them an opportunity to pretend they weren't racists, smiling White Lightnings gathered around him and shook his hand and slapped his back. They all drank beer and after a while a White Lightning went outside to the parking lot for a box of cigars from his saddle pack and ran back in screaming: "Some son of a bitch lacerated our new tires!"

Bull immediately realized that he could use their rage to his advantage. "I did it," he told them. "I fucked up your macho machines before I came in. I figured I'd do you a favor. You dudes look like you could use some exercise, so now you can walk."

Two White Lightnings sitting on either side of Bull at the bar were angry enough and stupid enough to attack him, and two quick punches, one with each hand, the old one-two, laid them out cold. After fifteen or twenty seconds every White Lightning in the place lay bloody and unconscious on the floor.

"I've seen some fights," Mini said, "but I never saw anything like that. It was so fast I could hardly tell what happened until it was over. Like watching a speeded up movie. Bull explained to me afterwards that when people lose their minds in anger they're easiest to deal with."

Bull came back from the creek drying his hands on his pant legs. "They'd already told me what we need to know," he said. He checked his watch. "Those bounty boy dudes with their mutts are supposed to meet up with what's left of the White Lightnings right here a little over an hour from now. Zouch has off-duty cops showing up too."

"It was Dipple who did their tires," Otro said. "There's hope for that boy."

"Zouch's stooge?"

"I'm sure he did it. He knows he belongs to the wrong tribe. I think he wanted his own forgiveness. You should leave now," he told Mini.

"What should I do?"

"Go on home and stay safe."

"Should I tell Loot anything?"

"Nothing. Not even that you saw me. Please don't say anything to Alejandro either. Don't say anything about Bull or me to anybody. Go on now. We'll see you soon. I promise."

"When? Where?"

"At the tavern when this is over with."

Mini smiled with worry in her eyes. "Adios," she said.

"Adios, Amiga cercana."

"Au revoir, bonne dame," Bull said with a smile. "I knew a fine French woman once, a genuine lady, back when I fought there. I learned some words, even a few simple sentences."

As she turned toward the parking lot Mini smiled with some of the worry gone.

"I stole a bottle of whiskey from your storage room," Otro called after her. "I'll pay you later."

"On the house!" she called back.

mini

She grew up on a small farm. Her father was a white man, a combat veteran wounded in action in his second war, and her mother was a refugee from Venezuela.

The father's wound was gastrointestinal, and, due to infections, healing of the mucosa, submucosa and serosal layers failed. After his medical discharge he did paperwork, as best he could, as much as he could handle, at a car repair shop. He was so emaciated by then that his nickname had become Bones.

The year before Mini started school Bones died in a tavern in town. Three customers, middle-aged men, claimed that he seemed drunk, went crazy, and came at them with a hunting knife. The truth was that the three customers were drunk, and one of them called Bones' wife a bean-chomper, and when Bones cursed him back all three dragged him into the men's room and beat him to death with their fists. Bones had gone to the tavern alone to sip a non-alcoholic beer while watching a college football game. The officially documented story was that he freaked out when his team fell behind and attacked three innocent victims in the men's room with a hunting knife. All seven men drinking at the bar, and one woman, as well as the bartender, corroborated the story. Nobody explained how these witnesses saw what happened in the men's room. Nobody ever found a hunting knife, or any knife, and nobody looked for one. Ten years later Mini's mother died of pancreatic cancer. Soon after her mother's death Mini met her magical mechanic, Alejandro.

Mini couldn't have defined "prodigy" or "savant," but both words could have rightfully been applied to her. She began to draw soon after she took her job running the tavern, thinking of it as a pleasant way to pass the many quiet hours she spent alone there. Her first few portraits of customers were done by memory in pencil on the sides of cardboard boxes. Because she wondered whether the drawings caught the likenesses she wanted, she showed them to Loot, who clearly saw what was there. Each portrait, though simply done, recorded the complexities of a distinctive human life.

Because she wanted to protect Mini, Loot hadn't yet told her, and might not ever tell her, that she possessed rare talent that came from unknown and mysterious sources. Loot thought she might show Mini's work to Gold and Sand. She thought she probably should, probably would. But there could be no assurance that anyone who mattered in the world of commercial art would recognize Mini's talent. If someone did recognize it, money and sycophantic praise might destroy both her gift and the contented life she lived within it.

otro

As they watched Mini drive away, Otro saw her portraits in his mind.

"Hey, man," Bull said. "Tell me your story now."

"Story?"

"Nobody knows shit about you. Don't hold back on me, man. Nobody knows who the hell you really are."

"There's a logical reason for that."

"What?"

"I don't know myself."

"What?"

"I'm not certain who I am. What I am. So I can't convince myself that it matters. We're all the same. Or should be. Or should at least try to be."

"Don't hold back on me, man."

"Will you keep it to yourself if I tell you what I know?"

"Do it. Please."

"I'm fairly sure my mother came from Asia. I'm almost sure my father was descended from a Tarahumara."

"Those Mexican distance runner dudes in that canyon."

"Yes. The Copper Canyon. What I'm certain of is that my mother died of cancer and my father killed himself. After that I was raised by poor white foster parents. I've always assumed they took me on because it brought them money. Not much, but more than they were used to. Money they needed. They lived and worked on a small dairy farm on worse than marginal land. I was young, six or seven, when they put me to work with them. Young as I was I realized they had no reason to love me. I never had the feeling they liked me much. But I made one friend, a girl my age from a nearby soybean farm. When I was ten she started bringing me books. I learned to read and write. When we were thirteen the two of us became lovers. I hated to leave her, but I did, about a year later. By then I'd read things that made me want to see the world. I felt I *had* to see it. Since then I've been on my own. I worked my way all over this country and after that a lot of the rest of the world. I've known people and learned their languages. I finally ended up here."

"How old are you?"

"Somewhere close to thirty."

Bull held his clenched fists up close in front of his face, as if to examine them. "Goddamn," he said as he dropped his arms to his sides. "How many people know what you just told me?"

"Only Loot."

"Thanks for telling me. Thanks, man. I've seen plenty of the world too. If things get much worse here we could cut out, see more of it together."

"I think I've seen enough."

Bull shook his head and smiled. "I hear you, man."

They walked back up the hill to wait, but not for long.

"Here they come," Otro said.

"I hear them," Bull said. He looked at his watch. "Ahead of schedule."

The White Lightnings came into view.

"Only seven left," Bull said.

"They're running out of people. Tires too, probably."

"Looks like this bunch is armed though."

The White Lightnings parked in the lot, walked into the park, and sat at the picnic table closest to the fire pit.

"I'll go down there," Otro said.

"Think you'll need me?"

"No. All I want to do is listen in. See that rounded boulder between the dead pines?" Otro pointed. "Wait for me behind the boulder. Water Eagle at the creek."

Bull led Eagle up the hill as Otro made his way to Modoc Park. He concealed himself in a willow thicket halfway between the remains of the outhouse and the table where the White Lightnings sat.

"Know what the worst is? I'm ashamed a giant nigger got the best of our men. It's a dis*grace!*"

"Where'd he come from? How'd he get here? How'd he get so fucking *big*? Who *is* he?"

"He's one giant black dude, that's all, that's who."

"He's in with that other, that weird desperado. Got to be."

"We'll get both the motherfuckers."

"I'll tell you something, Skyler. You don't talk a lot like a bank president."

"I'm not at the bank. I can talk any way I want out here."

"Amen!"

"A-fuckin'*men!*"

When the van arrived the seven White Lightnings hurried to the parking lot to meet the bounty boys and walk with them back to the park. As always, the dogs in the van howled and whined.

Now the White Lightnings wore holstered sidearms while the bounty boys, in camouflage gear and black boots, had long guns with scopes strapped over their shoulders. One of them walked with a limp, another carried a small silver flask, and the third sported a black snake tattoo that ringed his white neck.

The ten men gathered around the table, some sitting and some standing, and their talk began with a dispute between a White Lightning in a cowboy hat and the bounty boy with the snake tattoo:

"There's a big one coming," snake tattoo said.

"Big what?" asked cowboy hat.

"Big storm. Weather's fucking up again."

"Exactly what's that to us? And don't feed us any climate change bullshit."

"I said *big*. Remember the one two years ago?"

"No, man, that was three years ago."

"Bullshit. Two."

"Three."

"Two years, so shut the fuck up. You remember how many people got killed, no matter how many years ago it was?"

"Got killed where?"

"Right here's where."

"Right where?"

"Right here in this area. Right around here. Near here. Not too far away. You remember how many?"

"No I don't."

"One-hundred-and-twelve."

"Not that many. No way."

"It was one-hundred-and-fucking-twelve."

"Out of how many?"

"How many what?"

"How many people *live* in this area? How many people lived in this area three years ago? And anyway, what the fuck is an area? How big is an area?"

"It was two years ago."

"Well then how many people lived in this area two years ago?"

"What fucking difference does it make?"

"Big difference. Huge. Look at last year, okay? Last May. In some Florida hick town more than a hundred people died in a hurricane, right? So how many people lived in that town? About two thousand, right? So how many people lived in this area two years ago? One-hundred-and-twelve got killed out of how many?"

"You need to know the exact figure?"

"I want to know *about* how many at least. The approximate figure at least. It's the percentage that counts, it's how many out of how many. It's a legitimate factor, am I correct? And where'd you hear about this big storm anyway? And here's another question. How come you're so crude? So vulgar? So obscene? Explain *that.*"

"Who claims I'm vulgar?"

"Listen to yourself."

"Words aren't vulgar unless we believe they are. A word's a word. You have only one irrational reason for classifying a word as vulgar. By not using the word, you feel superior to the people who do use it. When you call me vulgar, all you're really doing is admitting to your own insecurity – your need to feel superior for no logical or healthful reason. So fuck you."

"Both you two do us all a favor," the silver flask bounty boy said. "Shut the fuck up! The point is, the only important point is, we don't have much time."

After the arguing stopped, silver flask outlined plans as to how they would either capture or kill the desperado who called himself Otro and kill his giant nigger sidekick too. A few White Lightnings would patrol the roads while the others burned the desperado's house down. Before they set the fire they'd take some of his clothes to give the dogs a fresh scent. The dogs would make ever widening circles and sooner or later strike the scent and the chase would be on. This time the end result would be many armed men chasing down no more than two.

A White Lightning interrupted: "So even if we get us a fresh scent, how we going to actually catch them? That barefoot son of a bitch can run!"

"But the big dude can't."

"Who says they'll stick together?"

"Back to the point," silver flask said. "We have provisions. We're going to *get* provisions is what I mean. Sheriff Zouch's delivering provisions right here, any minute now, and he's contracted reinforcements, and he's bringing them along too. We can chase after those two for as long as it takes. If we know where they are, or even *about* where they are, that's good enough, sufficient. Zouch's got communication. He can even bring in air surveillance unless the weather gets seriously fucked. So relax. We're out here to have us some fun. Maybe enhance our reputations. Look at it that way. Some fun along with payback and prestige."

Dark clouds hung low and Otro felt the temperature dropping. Rain would intensify a scent and help dogs track but truly heavy rain would wash scent away.

He hurried back to join Bull behind the boulder between the pines.

the white lightning in a cowboy hat

He changed his name to Gary Clint when he turned sixteen, his earliest legal opportunity. The name had been chosen at age fourteen, two years after he discovered, and soon became obsessed with, movies depicting the old American west.

"The Great Train Robbery," filmed in 1903, got him started. Other early westerns he admired included "Bronco Billy's Redemption," "Geronimo's Last Stand," "Shotgun Jones," "The Heart of a Bandit," "The Golden Bullet," "Wild and Wooly," and "The Rustlers."

Gary remembered the precise plots and major themes of those and dozens of other westerns, and had memorized every word of dialogue from his favorites, all produced in the second half of the 20th century. These films included "Shane," "The Outlaw Josey Wales," "The Magnificent Seven," "High Noon," and "Unforgiven."

"High Noon," starring Gary Cooper, and "Unforgiven," starring Clint Eastwood, were his top two, thus the name he chose to give himself.

Gary Clint believed that the old west had been the last place on earth where a man could be, or become, an authentic man, and that the old west was the last place where a human male on planet earth could truly be free. Riding through wild and dangerous country, entering an unknown town and walking into a crowded saloon, watching yourself throw down shots of straight whiskey in front of a mirrored bar, defending yourself with your fists, facing an armed adversary on a dusty street, frequenting a sanitary whorehouse, all of this was long gone and would never return. Gary Clint had no way of knowing how long he might live but he knew that he'd gladly trade half the years he had left to be transported back in time to, say, the late 1800s, when, in "Unforgiven," Clint Eastwood, as William Munny, won a gunfight against all odds and killed the town sheriff, Little Bill, who fully deserved it. In contrast, no 21st century man would ever win a fight against a hurricane, a flood, a wildfire or tornado.

Gary Clint had paid $9,017.99 for his chinchilla cowboy hat with its kangaroo leather sweatband, cattleman's crown, and diamond-studded hatband with a gold buckle, and he proudly wore it everywhere – to his work as a transportation engineer, to restaurants and wineries, to concerts, to his daughter's dance recitals, to his country club, and to Easter and Christmas church services.

To suggest that despite wearing an extravagant hat he remained a rugged, plain-spoken man – a modern day but genuine cowboy of sorts - Gary incorporated earthy figures of speech into his spoken vocabulary. Upon entering his favorite business district cocktail lounge after work on a stormy day he might tell the first acquaintance he ran into that "It's raining out there like a cow pissing on a flat rock." In his office, when he felt the occasional need to disparage an underling's work, he'd conclude that the employee in question was "as use-less as tits on a boar hog." The mannerism gained favor for him nearly everywhere.

otro

Bull cantered Eagle as Otro ran alongside. Warm rain began to fall before they were halfway to Otro's. Cross-ing Jump Off Joe Creek, Otro enjoyed the cool water soaking his legs and the smooth pebbles sliding under-neath his calloused feet. Eagle splashed across beside him. Jump Off Joe might reach flood stage before dark. Beyond the creek they came to a logging road through tall sugar pines. Otro made a mental game of kicking the big cones that lay scattered over the road. He award-ed himself two points for kicking a cone all the way off the road and one point for merely kicking it out of his way. He called a time out when he reached one hundred points.

"I wonder how many thousands of miles of logging roads there are out here," he yelled.

Bull changed the subject. "I married Ashes," he yelled back.

"In a church? In a courthouse?"

"That stuff doesn't matter."

"Loot and I are married the same way."

"Since when?"

"Neither of us know exactly when. But we are."

"We got to celebrate. Have us a party, the four of us."

"When the time's right, for sure."

They left the road when it turned west and soon crossed a barren ridge within sight of Otro's dwelling. When the first gust of warm wind slammed against them Eagle stopped in his tracks and lowered his head, and Bull slid to the ground. Both men sheltered behind the horse.

"Holy shit!" Bull yelled.

Otro barely heard him over the wind. His mouth inches from Eagle's left ear, he yelled, "Go! Go! Go!"

Eagle started down the hill, plodding slowly, one hoof at a time, head bowed low. Otro pressed both hands against Eagle's warm, wet hide with Bull close behind him. Intermittent windblown limbs from dead trees across the road sailed over their heads. When a small limb thumped into Eagle's foreleg he shuddered and dropped to his front knees, then raised himself and kept walking.

"Good boy!"

More than halfway down the hill the wind abruptly stopped.

"Slow!" Otro said. "Easy!" He patted Eagle's neck and jogged the rest of the way ahead of Bull and the horse. Along his way he counted six dead sparrows impaled on the thorns of star thistle plants. Across the road trees were down and the road itself was littered with limbs and branches. Suddenly the roaring wind came again and this time hit them from behind.

They circled the dwelling to escape the wind. Otro saw that Eagle's left knee had swollen. If the wind changed direction again the horse would know enough to use the dwelling as a shield.

Otro looked at Bull and pointed at the stairs, and Bull started up. Otro talked to Eagle and patted his rump, then climbed the stairs. Inside, Bull was on his knees arranging kindling in the woodstove. "How bad will it get?" he asked. He took a match from the cup on the floor beside the stove to light the kindling.

"If it doesn't let up we can stay the night."

"Do you figure it to let up?"

"Yes. It can't stay like this for very long."

"Then what?"

"Most likely heavy rain. Or there could be hail."

Harsh wind came and went. The duration of calm interludes lessened incrementally and each time the wind came it was stronger than the time before. Otro and Bull sat on opposite sides of the woodstove, ate smoked fish and dried fruit, and drank water and talked. Bull watched the road through the front window and Otro watched the wooded hills out back.

"Eagle's in the right place," Bull said.

"He's been through this before."

"This bad?"

"Yes. But not often."

"Holy shit," Bull said.

"What?"

"Here comes a sheriff's SUV weaving around all the crap on the road."

The wind recommenced with a roar.

"The son of a bitch stopped straight below us!" Bull yelled.

Otro looked down at the vehicle on the littered road and because of the wind he couldn't hear the automatic rifle fire but saw the muzzle flashes. Eagle stiffened, wobbled, dropped to his front knees and finally toppled onto his right side. When the flashes stopped and began again Eagle's body shuddered. His right foreleg twitched and stopped. A straight line of exit wounds reached from the base of his neck to his hindquarters. The belly-wounds oozed blood.

"We don't know who's in that thing or how many," Otro said. "Or what weapons they have. But I don't think they can get the angle they need to hit us up here."

"I hope they come up."

"They can't until the wind stops."

Otro and Bull sat across from one another at the kitchen table. The wind grew louder and tree limbs crashed into the back wall. Then more rain came. At the table, during the rain, they were close enough to talk with raised voices.

Bull asked Otro, "What's the highest wind speed ever?"

"Over two hundred miles per hour. Well over."

"In a hurricane?"

"A tornado."

"You figure it for two hundred out there now?"

"No."

Bull walked to the window to look for the SUV but couldn't see as far as the road through the downpour.

Eagle, barely visible, was half submerged in a widening stream.

"You keep tequila here?" Bull asked.

"Yes."

From a shelf next to the sink Otro took two tall Mexican shot glasses in one hand and a half-full bottle of Tres Generaciones in the other. He placed them on the table and sat down.

Bull held the three-quarter-liter bottle up by the neck to read the label. The bottle looked tiny in his huge hand. "Prime stuff," he said. "I took up tequila after I quit the cage." He uncorked the bottle, sniffed, then poured a shot glass half full. As he handed the bottle to Otro he sipped from his glass. "Bueno," he said. "Delicioso."

Otro poured his glass half full and set the bottle between them. "What did you use before tequila?" he asked.

"Mostly weed. What do you mostly use?"

"Peyote, but not often."

"I hope Loot's safe," Bull said.

"I hope Ashes is," Otro answered.

"We put the yurts on high ground in an east-west valley. They'll get some wind, but not like here."

Otro sipped his tequila and kept it in his mouth and held the shot glass up. "Yes," he said after he swallowed. "Delicioso."

"Life's bearable anywhere anytime with a slice of lime and a few grains of salt and tequila," Bull said with a smile. "But who needs lime and salt?"

The wind slackened and rain pounded down.

"People got to be dying out there," Bull said. "If my people need shelter, there's a safe cave near our camp. You've been there. It's high enough up for the worst floods."

"This place is safe. Loot's is too."

An explosion shook the cabin and an orange flash momentarily lit the room. A water glass and two plates fell from a shelf and shattered on the floor. The tequila bottle overturned on the tabletop and before much had spilled Bull set it upright.

Through the window all Otro could see was rain. "They can't be sure we're here," he said. "But maybe they saw some chimney smoke, maybe they know somebody's here. They want to flush us out. But they have to stay where they are for now. So do we."

"You sure they can't get us from the road?"

"They can't quite get the angle they need." Otro poured both shot glasses half full. "There won't be more than four men in an SUV. Most likely one or two. If anybody comes out armed we'll leave through the back."

"You got weapons?"

"Knives and bows."

"I got hands and feet."

"Whoever's down there doesn't have anything we need or want. We'll be all the way up the hill and into the trees before they get anywhere near us."

"I'll stay here," Bull said. "I can't run like you can. I'd slow you down. I can take care of business right here."

"Prost," Otro said. "That's what my friend Gold says when we drink."

"Prost back to you," Bull said.

They clinked glasses and sipped tequila.

"Prost," Bull said. "I've heard that word before, used it a few times myself, but I don't know exactly what it means."

"It's German, but its root is the Latin word prosit, meaning something like let-it-be-good."

"Let it be good," Bull said, and they clinked glasses again. "I suppose we could die in this."

"We could. Any important regrets?"

Bull took another sip. "No," he said. "We've been alive a while. One thing though. I wonder about it sometimes. Do you wish you'd lived in another time?"

"I wish I'd lived earlier."

"How much earlier?"

"Two, three hundred years."

"Me too," Bull said, and then laughed aloud. "I'd wish about two hundred too. But wish in one hand and shit in the other and see which one fills up first."

The rain stopped. They hurried to a front window. The SUV hadn't moved and was two feet deep in flood-water now. Eagle had disappeared underwater.

Then hail came hard with the stones splashing into puddles and streams and bouncing off the roof. They sat back at the table and Bull poured more tequila. "Prosit," he said, and they sipped from their glasses.

"Maybe we shouldn't drink much more," Bull said, "but I like the sound of the word. Prosit."

"Prosit," Otro said.

They clinked glasses.

"They might have a hard time just climbing out down there," Otro said. "When they do make it out they'll have a harder time getting anywhere."

When the hail abruptly stopped they walked to the window. Two deputies wearing head-to-toe battle gear and carrying weapons were wading slowly from the SUV toward Otro's driveway.

"Here they come," Otro said. "No hurry, but it's time. Out the back."

"Like I said, you go," Bull answered. "I'll deal with these two."

Otro made no argument, and they shook hands.

"See you soon," Bull said. "Sometime somewhere."

>-•-◄

Otro made his way up the hill toward cover. The air had turned cold, and he was slowed by fallen limbs and slippery hailstones under his feet. When he knew he was safe he stopped long enough to look back. The land was white with hailstones and a thin line of white smoke rose from his chimney. He liked the taste of Tres Generaciones in his mouth. He heard a scream from below followed by two muffled thuds that sounded to Otro like two men bouncing off a wooden wall.

He made the long trek to the cave. There were many downed trees to clamber over or circumvent. Halfway there he came upon a black-coated coyote feeding on a ruffed grouse. The animal, bloody feathers stuck to its muzzle, raised its head to stare at him.

To reach the mouth of the cave Otro used the escape route the bounty hunters had created after he'd trapped them behind a barrier of trees and limbs. Inside the cave he had more than enough food, water and wood for the night. Once he was warmed by his fire he explained to the skeletons how lucky they were to have lived on earth when they did. He told them that as long as he lived, they lived too. When he said goodnight and bent to touch the hand of the child the delicate bones fragmented underneath his fingertips.

Otro dreamed of the time he and his friend Carlos had made their camp on an empty beach between two sand dunes on a Pacific beach in Mexico. In the morning they set out at first light in a small wooden boat to watch for flocks of gulls or pelicans or a frigate bird or two diving for sardines driven to the surface by schools of feeding fish. They trolled all morning without hooking anything or sighting working birds. Near midday a pair of porpoises surfaced alongside to ride their bow wake and after that, as they headed toward shore, a high-flying pair of frigate birds off to the south suddenly set their wings and dove toward clouds of sardines breaking the calm surface. By the time Otro and Carlos got there pelicans and gulls were diving too. When Otro hooked a big bull dorado Carlos cut the motor. When Otro had played the fish up to the hull of the boat he handed his rod to Carlos. He reached to hold the dorado by the wrist of the tail with his left hand and then reached with his right to twist the hook from the fish's mouth. But as he lifted the dorado out of the water and swung it toward the boat it spit a live sardine from its mouth onto the panga floor. As the sardine flopped on the floor the thrashing dorado slipped from Otro's left hand and dropped back into the sea. The live sardine was hard to grasp but Carlos finally cupped it in both hands and dropped it over the gunwale. For a long time the two men talked about it. They knew they'd witnessed something with meaning but couldn't decide exactly what the meaning was. When Otro awakened after his dream he knew he'd never know the answer and knew he should be glad.

>-<

Otro spent three days and two nights in and around the cave. The daytime weather held sunny and warm. On the first afternoon he hunted blue grouse with stones. After searching likely cover for an hour he flushed a lone bird from a small elderberry patch. When the cock bird landed on a nearby limb Otro killed it cleanly with a head shot. He gutted and skinned the grouse, carried it back to the cave and broiled the lean meat slowly over a small fire. As darkness fell on that first day he wrote on the cave wall with charcoal –

> *Loot - if you find my words after I'm gone these are things I know. We respect each other and belong together. When we look at the world we see and understand what's there. Whatever we're made of we're the same. Because we hope to live with each other we don't want either life to end.*

If we live we'll continue to enrich each other. Whatever strength and courage I have I owe to you.

Early on the morning of the third day Otro indulged his compulsion to run.

He made his way down the mountain and took a well-worn game trail eastward through an expanse of fir. Running at a six-minute mile pace to warm up, he soon reached open country where, decades ago, hillside farms and orchards had drawn their irrigation water from a concrete ditch. Otro knew a place along the remains of the ditch where deer often bedded down. Running over wet earth that was hard-packed and firm, he picked up a good-sized stone and tossed it into a probable willow thicket. Wings drumming, a covey of valley quail burst from the cover and scattered. Seconds later a young whitetail buck came out behind the quail and started south. Otro watched the raised tail, the white rump and springy gait, and increased his pace and soon gained ground. The buck jumped the ditch with a single bound and stopped long enough to look back. Otro saw the buck's chest heaving, his legs trembling.

He followed the buck past the remains of a ramshackle abandoned house to a narrow, brushy draw that reached a mile eastward to another old homestead site. He thought the buck might jump the narrow draw, but it hesitated, then made a wheeling turn and started up the draw instead. All that was left at the homestead site was a long-neglected apple orchard with gnarled trees that bore fruit. Otro thought the buck would head there now if that was a place where he'd been feeding. The orchard was more than a mile up the draw but Otro cut the distance in half by running up a steep hill and down the other side. Downhill to his right, he kept the buck in sight most of the way.

By the time it was halfway up the hill the buck had slowed. Deer were sprinters, not distance runners, and its gait wasn't springy now and its head had lowered. Otro reached the crest of the hill and had to slow on the downhill side so as not to reach the orchard first. Twenty minutes later the animal was exhausted. The orchard made it easy. The buck didn't want to leave it, and each time Otro frightened it out of the apple trees it made a wide, nervous arc and then entered them again.

Finally the buck stood trembling, too exhausted to move. Otro had circled the orchard eleven times, keeping close in, while the buck in its wider circles had covered miles. Now it stood about twenty yards out from the orchard's west edge, facing west and looking back at Otro, who had slowed to a walk. The buck took a tentative step and its head sank, and Otro stopped where he was and talked to the animal soothingly.

When a minute had passed the buck's trembling had eased and then it raised its head. Otro walked up close enough to touch its warm, sweaty flank. The buck started away at a walk, head turned to watch Otro. When its eyes left Otro's it seemed to study the country. Finally it circled back to the draw and this time crossed it, then headed south and was soon out of sight.

Otro felt the power of wildness on the hand that had touched the deer. All of the apples had been eaten from the lowest branches of the trees, so he had to jump **to** get one. The fruit was hard, sour and delicious. When he finished the apple he ran back to the cave, where he took what he needed, ran home, and arrived before dark.

His dwelling was burned to the ground. Layers of wet ash in black and varying shades of gray surrounded the river-stone chimney. Wisps of pallid smoke rose from the ash and drifted south in warm wind. His Bronco was gone. Eagle, lean body bloated, lay dead near the bottom of the driveway.

Sheltered by trees but close to the road, Otro ran through the gathering darkness toward Mini's. His footfalls and deep breathing kept him from hearing the van with four armed teenagers in it coming up the road behind him. On each side of the van there was one boy with a shotgun and the other a rifle.

Rangbo, Stever, Chuckaluck, Rigor and Mortis visited the zone to fire their weapons twice a month. They took turns driving and placed restrictions on the games they played, and today had agreed to fire periodic thirty-second fusillades at fifteen minute intervals, and otherwise to hold fire until they saw either birds or animals to let loose at, or movements that suggested living creatures among the trees or in brushy cover. They were on their way home after a long day during which they'd recorded four certain kills: a turkey vulture feeding on a possum had been blown to bloody bits by semi-automatic rifle fire. A young coyote, staring at them from the roadside, had nearly been decapitated, its body riddled with magnum shotgun pellets. Two jack rabbits crossing the road together had also been taken down by shotguns. There'd been seven unauthenticated possibles.

"Possible to the left!" Chuckaluck, driving at the time, yelled loudly enough to be heard through the shooters' polyurethane earplugs. "Between the big trees!"

A rifle loosed dozens of rounds and a shotgun boomed six times.

"What the fuck was it?"

"Too dark! Who the fuck knows?"

When he heard Chuckaluck yell Otro had dived to the ground as rifle rounds smacked into nearby tree trunks and dozens of magnum pellets buzzed over his prone body and four of the pellets penetrated his right thigh.

⟶•⟵

Otro used his t-shirt to bind his wounds tightly over his bloodied pant leg. Before limping into Mini's he saw his friends through the front window – Gold, Sand, Alejandro and Mini.

"What the hell happened?" Sand asked.

"I'm shot."

"We heard shots. We heard somebody drive by. How bad is it?"

"Not so bad. A shotgun. My hamstring."

They were at a table next to the bar. Along with the chessboard, a dozen or more brown bottles sat on the table. Gold had the black chess pieces and as always he was winning. He hurried as best he could to get a chair from another table for Otro.

"Pull your pants down," Sand said. "I'll need some warm, soapy water. If you can, stretch your leg out straight."

Otro stretched his leg out.

As Sand examined the leg Mini brought a pail of water, and with it a double shot of tequila.

"Gracias," Otro said.

"Por nada, amigo."

While Sand worked on the thigh wounds and the others watched Gold told Otro the news: Down south people had died in the freak storm. Another violent storm was gathering here. Within thirty-six hours, ten to fifteen inches of rain with dangerously large hailstones would probably reach them. Floods would be widespread with wind reaching velocities of 60 to 80 miles per hour. Refugees from floods farther south had entered the vicinity ahead of the storm. From among the refugees, Loot was sheltering two young couples.

The two cops Zouch had sent to Otro's dwelling were beaten not quite to death by Bull, and later rescued by two more men Zouch sent. Those two had set Otro's dwelling afire and appropriated his Bronco. It was assumed that Bull had driven off in the first cops' SUV. No one had heard from or of him since.

"You'll be all right," Sand said to Otro. "Pellets passed through the muscle and missed the bone. I'll get you all cleaned up and bandaged. You'll be slowed down for a while. You'll heal well though."

Otro nursed his tequila and Mini told him about Loot. She had made careful plans before she met Zouch at his rally. Shortly before he was scheduled to speak she drew him aside to tell him she'd learned that a woman had been planted in the crowd to ask him to name an important issue he'd promote if elected. As Loot had hinted toward and hoped for, in his ignorant desperation Zouch asked her to suggest an issue. Certain he wouldn't know the word, she explained to him that a rumor relevant to a cherished freedom highly valued by country people – their kind of people - was spreading fast: radical liberal politicians, city people, wanted to outlaw the right of rural adults to practice necrophilia. She kissed Zouch's cheek, squeezed his hand, assured him he could trust her, and whispered in his ear that promoting necrophilia would be certain to win him votes. She kissed his lips and had him repeat the word until she was sure he had it memorized and could pronounce it. Then, kissing his lips, she briefly slipped her tongue into his mouth. She stepped back and squeezed his hand again and promised to celebrate with him in private after the rally, then turned and hurried away.

After a short speech containing the standard political clichés, Zouch volunteered to take questions. The friend Loot had planted in the crowd stood at once, waving her hand. She told Zouch that many voters she knew felt that he came across as a negative man, a law enforcement official who stressed punishing people but rarely if ever talked about helping them. For that reason she asked him to name something positive, a single worthwhile goal he'd work for if elected. Zouch smiled confidently and thanked her for the question and promised to do everything he could possibly do to protect the rights of hard working and patriotic Americans to have all the necrophilia they wanted.

The news that Zouch had publicly endorsed sex with corpses spread quickly. An aggressive newcomer who went by the name Nate Fury was certain to win the primary now, and then the general election. But Zouch would surely seek revenge on both Otro and Loot. As Sand worked on the leg wounds a group discussion concluded they should leave the area at once and stay away for at least three months.

>-·-<

Otro and Loot set out at daybreak the next morning. Neither of them divulged their destination to anyone. They would return to check conditions out in three months. The two young couples Loot had taken in were happy to serve as caretakers at her place.

Far to the north Otro knew a cave he'd discovered while guiding east coast hunters seeking trophy elk. In six days and nights, fighting wind, rain and hail, he and Loot covered more than one hundred miles through mountainous country, carrying as much as they could.

Otro's right hamstring, cleanly and securely wrapped, pained him every step of the way.

They created and organized life for themselves. Far from any remnant of alleged civilization, at an elevation of just over 6,000 feet, there was clean, cool air every day. When they cleaned their new dwelling thoroughly, Otro discovered the crudely carved wooden sculpture of a red, white and green elongated head wedged between two large rocks against a slab of tree bark far back at the darkest zone of the cave. He carried the relic out into the light and he and Loot admired the work and then carried it back to where he had found it and left it there.

They built a stone fire circle near the cave mouth, scavenged wood to make two chairs, a small table, and platforms for their sleeping bags. A nearby creek provided ample water. There were cutthroat trout in the creek, with healthy populations of grouse, mountain quail, rabbits and squirrels in the vicinity, as well as edible berries and plants.

Otro's leg was almost fully healed within a month. He and Loot hunted and fished and foraged for edible berries, seeds and roots. Loot cooked and Otro kept the cave and its contents clean and orderly. Loot had brought her brushes and made paint by mixing charcoal with animal fat. Inspired by Mini's work, she painted portraits from memory on all the walls. When she ran out of room on the walls Otro fashioned a stepladder. Long tree limbs served as rails and short ones as rungs, which were securely attached to the rails with vines. Now Loot could paint the ceiling. Otro predicted that her paintings would be discovered before a century had passed. On clear nights they sat outside together close to a small fire, under stars, planets, satellites, airliners and inevitable space junk. And the two of them were happy after their fashion.